Ground Faults

Ground Faults

A Lineage Series Novel

Michael Paul Hurd

Lineage Independent Publishing
Marriottsville, MD

ISBN (paperback): 9781958418109
First Printed in the United States

Publisher: Lineage Independent Publishing,
Marriottsville, MD

Maryland Sales and Use Tax Entity: Lineage Independent Publishing, Marriottsville, MD 21104

Contact: hurdmp@lineage-indypub.com

Website: https://lineage-indypub.com

To my grandchildren, William, Nolan, and Madelyn.

Ground Fault: when electricity takes an unexpected path to ground. If that path is through a human body, the resulting shock can cause severe injury or death.

CONTENTS

Chapter One: Beginnings
Starting Around 1900

"There are no rules here – we're trying to accomplish something."

Thomas Edison

* * * * *

"Oh, Archie! What happened to you?" Mrs. Thompson groaned as she saw her teenage son's bloodied nose and crimson-stained shirt. "This is the third time this month…" She paused for a moment to take in the situation. "And your glasses are broken, too!"

"Ma, it's nothing," Archie responded. "I'm just too smart for my own good sometimes. Everybody thinks I'm weird because of it. They call me 'four-eyes' and 'egghead' just because I spend time in the science lab with Mr. Morrison. He understands me."

"Never mind all that, Archie. Give me that shirt so I can start getting the blood out of it. We don't have the money for another one and if it sets, it will be impossible to get it all out," Mrs. Thompson said, her tone downplaying the importance of what her son had just said. She believed that hard work, not lots of time spent on "book learning," was the path to success. It had been her entire life and she knew no different.

Archibald Thompson, known to his family as "Archie" and later to his adult friends as "Sparky," came from a hardscrabble background of working-class families in Weehawken, New Jersey, across the river from New York City. Weehawken in general was a getaway location for the wealthy of New York City, but the part that the Thompson family called home was nothing more than a rat-infested slum. Sparky knew as he entered adolescence that his life would be better off somewhere else – despite what his own mother believed.

Sparky's father was rarely home. The elder Thompson toiled from dawn to dusk as a laborer, barely making enough to keep food on the table and a leaky roof over their heads. Sparky's mother did all that she could to keep the family together, even when her husband slipped into his periods of alcohol-induced melancholy.

Sparky was fortunate in that he had been taken under the wing of a respected science teacher at the local school. The teacher, Mr. Morrison, saw something – a spark of desire for knowledge – in young Archibald Thompson and began calling the young man "Sparky" whenever he was out of earshot of the other students, most of whom would be working on the digging of the New York City subway system by the time they were eighteen years old; some would even give up their lives for the effort.

Eventually, the other students heard Mr. Morrison call Sparky by that name and it stuck. He was no longer Archibald or Archie, just Sparky. It was sometimes used derisively, but Sparky didn't care. He would be leaving the godforsaken town once and for all.

Thanks to a glowing recommendation from Mr. Morrison, Sparky would spend the early years of his working life under the tutelage of Thomas Alva Edison in West Orange, New Jersey. He was assigned to a group of workers known as "Muckers."

The Muckers received working man's wages for a fifty-five-hour work week, regardless of their education or experience. Sparky saw first-hand how the wealth from Edison's recently approved patents flowed upward into the pockets of Edison and his rich investors, rather than the pay envelopes of the workers. The frenetic pace of the work, coupled with poor nutrition and bad lighting, left Sparky and most of his colleagues gaunt and sallow. They toiled from dawn till dusk most days, barely taking time to enjoy sunshine and fresh air.

Over time, the conditions took their toll on the men's health. Nearly all of them lost weight and more than a handful suffered from chronic respiratory infections. Others became recluses, returning to the mental and physical solitude of their meager accommodations at the end of their tiring workdays, only to repeat the cycle again the next day.

It was perhaps fortunate that most of the Muckers were unmarried or geographically separated from their wives. Some were recent college graduates, while others had left their farms behind in search of a living wage. Those men left their wives behind in the care of extended families. Over time, the lack of female companionship and influence showed: by Friday of each week, the factory floor and laboratories reeked of sweat and stale tobacco. In the summertime, the stench was particularly nauseating as most of the men had foregone regular bathing. Many thought they didn't need to bother, with no woman around to be presentable for.

Sparky had been with the Edison crowd for approximately three years when a series of accidents began.

Men were shocked, but not quite electrocuted. Others fell from low platforms and suffered broken bones. Still others endured slip-and-fall situations when small areas of the floors were "accidentally" polished with lard.

Edison's managers surmised that foul play was involved, but could never connect the unfortunate mishaps with even a suspected perpetrator. The only anecdotal connection was that Sparky always seemed to be nearby when a mishap occurred – but so were about a dozen other people. Any one of them could have had the opportunity to arrange the so-called accidents.

In his spare time, Sparky was a voracious reader of anything to do with electricity. He was particularly interested in the works of a University of Buffalo professor and dentist, Alfred Porter Southwick, who had died a few years earlier. Southwick was widely published in scientific journals and advocated the use of electricity to replace hanging for executions. Sparky paid particular attention to the mechanics of electrocution, especially how a person's body conducted electricity from a source to a ground.

Sparky was also a quick learner of electrical theory and the mechanics of wiring. He wired many homes and businesses in West Orange, working "off the books" on a cash basis separate from Edison's laboratories. After just a couple of years, he had developed enough skill and a broad clientele that would provide a safety net if he ever left the Edison factory.

Having those skills was fortunate, as Sparky had been an unwitting participant in a series of pranks within the Edison complex. That involvement, once discovered, brought an exit from Edison's employment sooner than Sparky had intended: Edison himself had demanded Sparky's resignation. Normally, such behavior would have resulted in dismissal for cause, but the allegations of Sparky's involvement were not proven – so Edison allowed Sparky to preserve his dignity and resign.

After resigning, Sparky kept in regular letter contact with his only friend there, a man who went by the name of John Garfield. It was Garfield who had masterminded many of the pranks, but his involvement was never confirmed, despite the suspicions of management. Instead, an embarrassed Sparky had taken the blame to protect his friend.

Garfield normally did not have a conscience, but Sparky had been his only friend at the Edison factory. A remorseful Garfield offered to provide Sparky with a supply of outlets and switches – as long as Garfield was kept apprised of where Sparky was living and working. Sparky saw the economic benefit that could result from Garfield's proposal.

Once out of West Orange, Sparky never spent more than six months in one place. At first, he relied on the good graces of others, barns, chicken coops, rooming houses, and greasy spoon diners for his survival. The money he earned, always paid in cash, was good; he merely elected not to spend any more than was necessary to meet his most basic needs. Thompson also made sure that he did not get emotionally entangled with any of the eligible women he encountered. It was all "just business" to him.

His popularity was growing, but Sparky suffered from a bit of a "Robin Hood Complex.' As he wired homes for electricity, he saw the disparities between the rich and working class. "The rich have everything," he would think to himself, "while the working man barely makes it from day to day." Thompson vowed that he would make it his life's work to ensure the common man got his due. He just wasn't sure how he would fulfill that goal.

Moving west across Pennsylvania, Sparky first stopped in Allentown. Industry was growing there, bringing with it a workforce who would need their homes wired for electricity. Thompson helped meet that demand. He wired several hundred craftsman-style homes for factory workers, as well as mansions owned by the wealthy industrialists of the city.

Adding electricity to the homes of working families became Archibald Thompson's pride and joy. He made sure their homes were safely wired and that they could be upgraded to the newest appliances, like the Hoover vacuum cleaner. "Anything," he thought, "to make the life of their overworked homemakers easier." Sparky also realized that most of the working families could more afford to pay for his skills in kind rather than in cash. Food was the currency of the poor; as he worked, Sparky's bony frame quickly filled out and his vision improved from the more diverse diet and improved living conditions overall.

Chapter Two: Allentown
1902

Nearing the end of his time in Allentown, Sparky was hired by one of the steel mills to electrify its plant so that it could more efficiently operate during the hours of darkness. The owner of the mill, Waldo Emerson Butler, also hired him to wire his mansion which stood on a hill overlooking the Lehigh Valley. It was during this extremely busy period that Archibald "Sparky" Thompson took on an apprentice, an Irish immigrant named Seamus Conaty.

Conaty, the epitome of a "red-headed Irishman," hailed from County Cavan in the Parish of Kilmore. He claimed that he had come to America with his wife, Bridgit, in hopes of finding respectable employment with a well-to-do family. Seamus recounted their existence in Ireland, tied to a small tenant farm that barely offered a subsistence output. "The Conatys," Seamus said, "were accustomed to the hard work and long hours that being in service to a wealthy family required."

Seamus Conaty, however, was not the ideal servant and had, since their immigration about three years earlier, continually gotten into disagreements with the head housekeepers and head butlers. He needed an employment situation that did not require his constant deference to those of a higher social standing. It was the opportunity to learn a skilled trade and eventually strike out on his own as a journeyman electrician that drew him to Archibald "Sparky" Thompson.

*   *   *   *   *

Steel tycoon Waldo Emerson Butler, named because of his mother's penchant for romanticist poets, made his fortune by being in the right place at the right time. Using a meager inheritance from his grandfather, Butler bought up the land needed for the early railroads at a mere fraction of their eventual value. He later sold the land to the Reading Railroad Company at a substantial profit, which he reinvested in steel mills and foundries that made the boilers for locomotives.

The Butler Mansion, completed in 1900, was a sprawling complex built in the popular Victorian style. Its lower floor held a formal reception area, a dining room large enough to seat fifty, and a few other smaller rooms and offices where quiet conversations between the captains of industry (or their wives) could take place uninterrupted and unmonitored. It lacked the ambiance of a formal library, instead featuring a conservatory where musicians could give mini concerts or writers could present their orations and recitations.

The second floor of Butler Mansion were devoted to bedrooms for the Butler children and a large master suite with separate sleeping accommodations for Waldo and his wife, Florence (nee Southwick). The third floor, with hidden stairways down to the second floor, lower-level kitchen and food preparation areas, held dormitory space for twenty domestic servants.

Waldo Emerson Butler had his mansion built from the ground up with indoor plumbing and running hot water. Even the servants' dormitories were equipped with modern plumbing and a flush toilet; however, it was sometimes a challenge for the servants all sharing that single bathroom. For that reason, the domestic staff maintained an outdoor privy in a grove about a hundred yards downhill of the mansion, to be used only in emergencies.

The Butler family, though, never lacked for a place to "take care of business," as each of the six bedrooms on the family level were *en-suite* with their own private flush toilet, bathtub and sink.

Wanting to surprise his family when they returned from their summer home in the nearby Poconos, Butler had arranged with Sparky to have the main home wired for electricity. Sparky would be "paid a handsome sum" if he had the entire first and second floor wired before the Labor Day holiday. It was a challenge that Archibald "Sparky" Thompson willingly accepted.

Butler went to great lengths to show Thompson the entire mansion, minus the servants' dormitories, of course. It was not Butler's style to simply grant his staff any additional amenities. They were, he said repeatedly, "Paid to work, not to lay about all hours of the night reading, if they could read at all, under electric lights." Sparky remembered these words as he began the work; Butler's condescending tone grated on Sparky. Understanding that Butler would never stoop so low as to visit the servants' quarters, Sparky took it on himself to wire them for electricity anyway, albeit minimally. That, he hoped would put him in the good graces of Mrs. Butler, who he had heard was a model mistress, always looking out for the welfare of the servants.

First wired was the reception area. There, Sparky installed a fancy overhead light fixture fitted with two dozen incandescent bulbs. It was operated by a single push-button switch in the center of the longest interior wall of the room. Sparky went from there to the rest of the main floor, ending in the kitchen.

"Mr. Thompson, a word if I may?" Butler asked as Sparky was finishing with the kitchen wiring on Thursday afternoon. "Are you certain you can be finished with the family quarters by noon on Monday? Mrs. Butler and our four children… adults now… will be returning from the Poconos on the morning train. They telephoned me just an hour ago with their itinerary."

"Yes, Mr. Butler. I have the entire weekend to do the work and with most of your household staff away for their own time off, it should not be a problem," Thompson replied.

"You've already seen the family quarters, my good man, so I will leave you to it," Butler said as he excused himself back to his now-illuminated office.

Back on the second floor, Sparky took in the opulence of the spotless family quarters. The mattresses and linens on the beds defied sensibility. Sparky could not resist the opportunity to flop down on the overstuffed mattress, hearing the starched and pressed linen sheets crackle under his weight. He was accustomed to sleeping on a horsehair mattress laid across a woven rope frame – a far cry from what he was now experiencing.

As he lay there looking up at the ceiling, Sparky's mind was racing. Here was his chance to right another wrong against the working men of Allentown. They worked themselves to death in the mills and factories, all the while padding the pockets of the wealthy industrialists. He hadn't presented Butler a final bill for materials, just an estimate for the required labor, and charging Butler premium prices for the wires, switches, outlets, and other hardware would give Sparky a cash cushion that he could pass on to the fledgling Laborers International Union of North America.

The writings of Marx and Engels had also gotten Sparky's attention. He recognized the dichotomy of Allentown society, where the few controlled the wealth while the many produced the goods and services that underpinned a booming economy. However, Sparky saw that none of the economic well-being was ever used for the improvement of the living standards of the workers. He felt compelled to do something about it.

Apprentice Seamus Conaty, on the other hand, knew that money would not always fix problems. There were other ways to get the attention of the rich and powerful that did not always make them dig deep into their wallets. Claiming that he was new to the electrical trade, Seamus absorbed information like a sponge and was quick, perhaps even quicker than Sparky had been, to master electrical theory and hardware concepts.

Sparky and Seamus worked madly through the next few days, stopping only for a bite to eat or a quick nap in the adjacent carriage house. They worked up from the cellar and the new fuse box that would eventually hook up to the main service line. First, there was the knob-and-tube wiring, then the branch lines to each room for the switches, outlets, and lights. It was tedious work, but Sparky and Seamus were on a mission.

By Monday morning, the job was finished. An exhausted and dirty Sparky walked Mr. Butler through the ground floor arrangements, including the kitchen. Butler quickly became bored with the details; he just wanted everything to work. They didn't ever get to the upstairs part of the job; Butler accepted on face value that the second floor living quarters were similarly wired. His corpulence made it difficult for him to ascend the stairs more than once a day without being left breathless.

"Mr. Thompson, I thank you so much for getting the job done on schedule. I shall write you a check for your services. Will a hundred dollars do?" Butler asked, the tone of his voice somewhat condescending.

"No, Mr. Butler. That estimated amount was based on standard grade materials," Thompson replied. "I took the liberty of using premium quality materials everywhere in your home, except, of course, the servants' quarters. As you instructed, they were not given full electric service nor the advantage of premium quality." Sparky had recognized early in the job that Butler would not oversee the quality of the components; Sparky's claim that they were "premium grade" would not be challenged. Butler's expertise was in steel and logistics, not electricity. Inflating prices and the quality of materials was the one unscrupulous practice that Sparky engaged in. Aside from this, his workmanship was always above reproach.

Butler was puzzled but did not argue the point. "What, then, is your final figure, Mr. Thompson?"

"I should think that five hundred dollars will cover the additional costs," Sparky replied, his face deadpan.

Sparky fully expected to be shown the door and stiffed for the additional amount; instead, he was being presented with a check from the richest man in Allentown. It was more than most men made in a month of working a standard sixty-hour week. After cashing the check and giving Seamus his wages, paying their rooming house accounts, and taking a small stipend for himself, Sparky was able to give nearly two hundred dollars to the Union's emergency fund.

Chapter Three: The Conatys
Beginning in Baltimore, ca. 1902

The *SS Chemnitz* had been anchored between Fort McHenry and Fort Carroll for over a week awaiting clearance from immigration authorities. An outbreak of louse-borne typhus (*Rickettsia prowazekii*) on board the ship had necessitated its quarantine before entering the Port of Baltimore. The overcrowded conditions had contributed to the outbreak, which was entirely in the steerage class. First-and Second-Class passengers, because of an enforced physical separation from steerage, were not affected by the body lice infestation.

Among those infected with typhus were Seamus and Bridgit Conaty. They, along with nearly fifteen hundred other passengers, had dormitory-style accommodations in the *Chemnitz*'s lower decks. The cramped conditions were compounded by an extremely rough crossing, leaving nearly all of the steerage passengers too seasick to even leave their three-high berths. First- and Second-Class passengers fared only marginally better because their conditions were not as crowded and fresh air was more readily available.

While the *Chemnitz* rode blissfully at anchor, the U.S. Lifesaving Service and Immigration officials sent boatloads of supplies to ensure that the passengers remained clothed, fed, and had sufficient drinking water. The same vessels returned to their stations loaded with the bodies of those who had passed away from the fevers of typhus. Over the two weeks that the disease ravaged the passengers on the crowded lowest decks, approximately twenty percent of them died.

The Conatys eventually recovered from their fevers and were delighted to be among the first steerage passengers cleared to go ashore after the *Chemnitz* docked at the Immigration pier. It was a cacophony of noise and unrecognizable languages. The sailing had originated in Bremen, Germany, so a good portion of the steerage passengers were from Germany and Eastern Europe. Immediately in front of Seamus and Bridgit was a German couple who, because they didn't speak English, were having trouble communicating with the Immigration officer.

The delay taxed Seamus's patience. Bridgit sensed his anxiety and placed her hand on his forearm in an effort to calm him. Seamus grumbled, "Weeks in a boat and now we feckin' wait again!"

"Aye, and if you don't get that Irish temper under control, Mr. Conaty, it won't be just Immigration you'll be waiting for!" Bridgit teased with a twinkle in her eye.

Finally, a German-speaking Immigration officer arrived after the line had been held up for several minutes. He helped the couple, in their fifties, get through the immigration questions:

"*Namen?*" the German speaker asked.

"*Fenstermacher. August und Klara,*" the husband responded.

"*Woraus kommen Sie?*" was the next question from the officer. For the records, he needed to know where the couple originated.

"*Wir kommen aus Russland,*" August Fenstermacher replied. They had originated from Russia.

"*Was ist deiner Ziel?* What is your destination?" The officer asked in German and English.

"Wir nehmen den Zug nach Michigan," Klara replied proudly. *"Unser Sohn trift uns dort."* They would be taking the train to meet their son in Michigan.

Seamus and Bridgit were next. They were asked the same questions in both English and German; the Immigration officer at the desk sighed in relief when Seamus answered in English. Seamus gave their names and country of origin, then said that they would be heading to Dundalk in hopes of finding family that had settled there. Seamus chose Dundalk only because it was named after its Irish counterpart, not because he really had any relatives there. He thought for a moment that it might be worth following the Germans to Michigan as they obviously had contacts there.

After passing the Immigration checkpoint, the men and women were separated and taken for delousing. Their clothing and baggage were fumigated with Cyklon-A, a form of hydrogen cyanide, while their naked bodies were dusted with delousing powder. Somehow, they managed to emerge with their dignity intact – or so it seemed.

The so-called privacy fences surrounding the women's delousing area were anything but private. The boards were riddled with knotholes through which prying male eyes could peer. The area between the fences was rarely patrolled by the authorities, so many an adolescent male got their first look at unclothed female bodies through those knotholes. One entrepreneurial young man recognized a business opportunity and started charging admission for a five-minute stint between the fences. Anyone caught giggling or making lewd sounds was quickly removed.

Seamus had been very observant through the entire process. He noticed that the First-Class passengers did not have to go through the delousing and merely strode ashore down the gangway. The Second-Class passengers were given similar treatment, except their heads and beards were first inspected for lice; only those found to be infested were shunted out of the line to the delousing station. Seamus swore that he would do whatever he could to deal with the inequitable treatment of people based on their wealth or social standing.

Taking the Number 26 streetcar, the Conatys were in Dundalk in a matter of minutes. They had enough money to spend a few nights in Dundalk's only rooming house for married couples. As they got their bearings and began adapting to life in America, the first requirement was finding work.

Seamus was the first to find employment, with the Canton Company. A couple of weeks later, Bridgit entered the employ of The Johns Hopkins Hospital as a laundress. The influx of money meant they could move to more permanent accommodations closer to both the hospital and the Canton complex on Boston Street. Being able to walk to and from their jobs was important. Streetcar fares were reasonable but relying on them for transportation at both ends of unpredictable workdays was an expensive and time-consuming proposition.

The accommodations alone were a significant upgrade. Their apartment was still small, but it was equipped with its own toilet and bathtub. They no longer had to share common facilities with a dozen other families. Bridgit, an absolute pillar of Catholic modesty, was relieved that she would no longer be subjected to the embarrassment of other men walking in on her during her bathing rituals

They had barely gotten settled in the upstairs apartment of their tenement rowhome when Seamus got into a bit of trouble. Because he was a newly arrived Irishman, everyone doubted his ability to complete complicated tasks. They called him "Mick" or "Paddy," both of which were usually prefaced with "dumb."

The incessant badgering was led by the shop foreman, Michael Murphy. It continued after the 5 o'clock whistle on Friday evening and spilled over into Seamus's walk home. Seamus had tolerated all that he could and suddenly lost his temper. In a blinding rage, Seamus grabbed Murphy by the lapels and forced him into a nearby alley. He simply had had enough.

Shoving Murphy away and spinning on the ball of his left foot, Seamus sucker-punched Murphy, a Baltimore native of Irish descent. The second bare-fisted punch dropped Murphy to the ground unconscious. Seamus's rage peaked and he began kicking the downed man mercilessly; the sounds of ribs breaking was sickening.

Before long, Murphy was bleeding from his mouth and nose, not from the punches, but from the repeated kicks that had caused irreversible internal damage. He gasped and gurgled, drowning in his own blood. His final breath was marked with the expulsion of bloody bubbles from his mouth and nose along with a loss of excretory control; the smell of urine and fecal matter quickly filled the immediate area, overpowering even the odor of the "alleyway toilets" used by men leaving the local bars.

Standing over Murphy's now-lifeless body, Seamus looked around to be sure there were no obvious witnesses and broke into a run as he fled the scene.

Reaching the main street, Seamus slowed to a fast walk and turned left then turned left again, looking over his shoulder to be sure he wasn't followed. As he made the second left, he ran squarely into a Baltimore City police officer. Seamus made eye contact and noticed that the officer had a raw wound on the left side of his face that was still healing, perhaps the result of a knife fight.

"Watch where you're going," the officer said sternly.

"I do apologize to ya;, officer. I believed I was being followed by a gang of shites," Seamus replied somewhat sheepishly, putting his hand on his chest. Wanting to emphasize the appearance of innocence, he touched the brim of his flat cap with two fingers and nodded almost imperceptibly to the officer.

"Be on yer way and be careful about it, too!" said the officer. Seamus picked up his determined pace and kept it just short of a run. It was a close call that he did not want to repeat. One thing that Seamus noticed was a little leftover Irish brogue in the officer's speech. "Could the officer be sympathetic to the Irish cause?" Seamus thought to himself.

Finally at their squalid apartment, Seamus found Bridgit mending his socks and humming an Irish tune to herself. Words flowed from his mouth faster than she could understand them. He was near panic.

"We… have to leave… now… I killed a man on the way home from work," Seamus said at a frenetic pace.

"My darling, slow down. I can't understand you," Bridgit replied.

"He's dead. He drowned in his own blood, I tell ya," Seamus explained. "All day long, it was 'dumb Mick' this and 'stupid Paddy' that. Then he followed me out of the factory. It was all I could take. We have to leave before anyone figures out what happened. We have two days to get outta here before they will miss him at work."

"Seamus, I promised to stick by you in thick and thin. Let me start packing up our things," Bridgit replied calmly. "I will also leave a note for the landlord, telling him that we had to go back to Ireland for family reasons. You know we can't afford it, but the landlord doesn't need to know how little money we have. If we tell him we've gone back to Ireland, the *poilini* will be thrown off our trail."

They were both hourly workers, so if they did not show up for work on Monday morning, their bosses would assume that they had quit. Available labor was at a surplus, so finding someone to replace the Conatys would not be a problem.

Heading for Camden Station with all their belongings in two suitcases and one steamer trunk, the Conatys had no idea where they should go. They knew that north was probably the best option. They could go to Philadelphia or New York, both of which had significant Irish populations, but neither of them wanted any part of big city life. Baltimore was more than big enough. Bridgit looked at the map on the wall at the station and decided that they should head for Allentown. It was a purely arbitrary decision.

They boarded the next northbound train that would pass through Allentown. On the six-hour journey that would reach Allentown before dawn, the couple hardly spoke and were too tense to sleep. Seamus was afraid that he would be overheard discussing details of the fatal fight and Bridgit did not want them to be subjected to any more bullying because of their Irish origin and accent.

They finally reached Allentown and found a place to stay. It was fortunate that they both had received their previous week's pay envelopes before Seamus's altercation. Without that money, the Conatys would have been destitute and likely would have resorted to begging. Settling into their room, they spoke in hushed tones.

"Seamus, it's just like it was in Ireland. Your temper is your devil and gets the best of you every time," Bridgit sputtered.

"I can't help meself," Seamus replied. "Anybody that insults me or my family will have to pay for it. It was the way I was brought up. My father allus wanted me to be a prizefighter, like the Gardner brothers, and he taught me how to fight."

"You need to find the nearest priest and make confession even before you find a job," Bridgit insisted. "You will be damned for all time if you do not repent and receive absolution for your mortal sin." She made the sign of the cross.

"Yes… my darlin', I've killed a man in anger and certainly that is a mortal sin," Seamus countered, hanging his head shamefully.

"We will not discuss the subject any longer once you have seen a priest," said Bridgit. Her tone was resolute, and Seamus knew better than to argue.

*　　*　　*　　*　　*

The incident in Ireland was at the Harland-Wolff shipyard in Belfast, where Seamus worked on ships destined to join the White Star Line's fleet just before their emigration to the United States. They had abandoned their small farm in County Cavan and headed northeast to Belfast, where there was always plenty of work, especially in the shipyard.

Ulster's County Cavan was, for the most part, dirt poor and unsuited for anything other than sheep grazing and subsistence farming. Seamus and Bridgit had a small holding that had, according to legend, been in Seamus's family for nearly a thousand years. That was not how they wanted to live their lives. Instead, they packed up, abandoned the farm, and moved to Belfast after reading in the newspaper that the Harland-Wolff shipyard was looking for laborers.

At the shipyard, unskilled laborers were sorted and assigned based on the shipyard's immediate needs. All applicants for one week might be assigned to riveting; the next week, the newest applicants could be split between plumbing and electrical work. Plumbing was nothing new in the shipping industry, but the use of dynamo-powered electricity had quickly spread around the world after the *SS Columbia* was fitted in 1880 under the personal supervision of Thomas Edison.

Seamus was assigned to the Harland-Wolff electrical team working on both the *SS Corinthic* and the *SS Ionic* for the White Star Line. He was not a skilled tradesman but absorbed information rapidly and was soon moved off the laborer team and onto the sub-apprentice team. Seamus was now responsible for much more than moving materials from place to place on the two ships and within the shipyard. He was actually connecting wires, albeit under the direct supervision of a journeyman or master electrician.

All was going well for Seamus, and he was able to provide Bridgit with much more than subsistence and a roof over their heads. His pay packet usually contained enough money to cover their weekly expenses and an evening out at the local pub just outside the workers' entrance to the shipyard. Seamus also allowed Bridgit to purchase a new frock for herself once a month. They were, or so Bridgit thought, a couple on their way up in the world.

The one thing she could not count on was Seamus's ability to control his temper, which flared uncontrollably for the first time in Belfast just less than six months after his first shift. Seamus had been harangued for a full day by an English foreman from Liverpool. The verbal abuse had crossed a line and ended up in a fist fight outside the shipyard gates. The foreman lived, but Seamus was brought to trial for assault. The Irish magistrate, himself of Irish descent, was sympathetic to Seamus's argument and did not impose a prison sentence.

Instead of prison, the Belfast magistrate gave Seamus a choice: he could return to County Cavan or leave the British Isles permanently. He was given the weekend to discuss the options with Bridgit and they chose emigration over returning to County Cavan. By Tuesday, the Conatys were on a ferry to Liverpool, then a train to Southampton, and from there on board the *SS Chemnitz* to Baltimore.

*   *   *   *   *

The Conatys had been in Allentown for only a couple of days before Seamus found a parish, St. Patrick's, and a priest who was hearing confessions. As he approached the confessional booth, Seamus was somewhat concerned that the priest would, after hearing his confession, call for the authorities to make an arrest. In Ireland, what was said in confession to one's priest was sacrosanct; this was his first confession in the United States, and he did not know what to expect or who he could trust. He had first-hand how Irish immigrants were treated in Baltimore.

As he waited to confess his mortal sin, Seamus even wondered if the body of the man he killed was still lying in the street. The image of the bright red blood bubbling from the man's mouth as he breathed his last haunted Seamus day and night. Most nights, he awoke from the same nightmare drenched in sweat. "Perhaps my confession will remove that ghost from my mind," he thought to himself.

Entering the confessional with nervous sweat now dripping from his brow, Seamus sat down. The screened door opened, and the priest began the Order of Confession, which Seamus joined in unison after making the sign of the Cross, "In the name of the Father, Son and Holy Spirit."

The priest continued, "May the Lord be in your heart and help you to confess your sins with true sorrow." Seamus was relieved to hear a hint of an Irish accent coming from behind the confessional screen.

Seamus smoothed his hair and took a deep breath. His heart was pounding as he began his confession. "Bless me, Father, for I have sinned," Seamus continued. "It has been six months since my last confession, in Ireland…"

Chapter Four: Baltimore's Finest...
1902

Meanwhile, in Baltimore not long after the Conaty's hasty departure, a Canton Company worker looking for a place to empty his bladder discovered Michael Murphy's lifeless body in a back alley not far from the entrance to the factory. The foreman's face had been beaten to a pulp and was barely recognizable, but there was enough that the passer-by could positively identify it as Murphy.

Sean Mulcahy was the first police officer to arrive. He took a statement from the worker and advised the man to remain on the scene until he was dismissed by the police. Another patrol officer took statements from anyone in the gathering crowd who had even the slightest bit of information. It turned out that the dead foreman was a tyrant and known for his capricious discipline and summary dismissal of even the most reliable employees. In other words, Michael Murphy was disliked and, in some cases, hated by his subordinates.

Mulcahy used one of the newly installed police call boxes to summon additional officers to the scene, including the Chief Coroner. The city's Chief Coroner estimated, based on the coagulation of the blood, that Murphy had been dead for at least twenty-four hours. Had it been in the heat of a Baltimore summer, putrefaction would also have set in; however, the cooler night temperatures kept that from happening. It was another fact that the Chief Coroner noted in his case file.

Turning to the man who reported finding the body, Mulcahy noticed that the man's knuckles were bruised and the skin broken open in more than one place. He also had blood spatters on the lapels of his jacket and the seam joining the sleeve of his coat to the body was torn. Mulcahy surmised that the man had recently been in a fight.

"I think you need to come down to the station house with me," Mulcahy said sternly.

"Why? I've done nothing wrong," the man replied.

"There are some details surrounding the dead man that we need to go over," Mulcahy said, trying to downplay his own suspicions. "If you will come along without any resistance, I can spare you the embarrassment of being frog marched past this crowd in handcuffs. What is your name?"

"My name is O'Brien. Nicholas O'Brien. I've nothing to hide. I did not kill Mr. Murphy."

Reaching the station, O'Brien was put in an interrogation room with his left wrist handcuffed to an eye bolt in the table. As he sat in the room, a rotating lineup of officers came and went, peppering him with questions, most of which were related to the discovery of the foreman's body. If the man dozed in the chair, a loud rap on the table by an officer's baton shocked him back into consciousness.

After about eight hours, Mulcahy grew impatient. He *knew* this Nicholas O'Brien was responsible for the foreman's death, but there was not enough evidence to prove the case. After midnight, Mulcahy took matters into his own hands, slamming his hands on the desk with enough force to make O'Brien flinch.

"We know you did it!" Mulcahy exclaimed as he pressed his face close to O'Brien's. Mulcahy's exhalations were vile with the repugnant odor of his partially-digested dinner of garlicky sausage and onions lingering in the air with each breath. Nicholas recoiled, holding his breath and hoping he would neither gag nor vomit.

When Mulcahy removed his police officer's tunic, the repugnant smell was exacerbated. It wasn't just his breath that smelled bad; it was his whole body. His perspiration-soaked undershirt reeked of garlic and onions, just like his breath.

"I don't know how Mr. Murphy was killed," O'Brien responded. "I just found him lying there when I was walking home from the bar across the street."

"Liar!" Mulcahy bellowed. He slapped the table with his open hand for emphasis.

"Please, sir… leave me be. I want to go home," Nicholas O'Brien groveled.

"You have blood on your coat. Your knuckles are bruised and broken, and your sleeve is torn. You've obviously been fighting," Mulcahy growled. "Come clean and we will make it easy on you. You won't get sent to the chair."

"I will not confess to something I dinna do. I can explain…"

Mulcahy stopped O'Brien in mid-sentence with an openhanded slap across the left side of his face. It was hard enough that tears quickly welled up in his eyes; he nearly fell off his chair from the force of the blow.

"Tell me the truth!" Mulcahy bellowed once again.

"I was attacked by some 'Eyetalians' on my way home from work. It was all I could do to get away from them," Nicholas tried to explain. "I tell ya, I fought off three of them!"

"Liar!" Mulcahy bellowed once again and followed his accusation with a slap to the other side of the man's face. "Tell me again why you have blood on your clothes."

"I just told you, Officer... I was attacked by some guys from Little Italy. I'm Irish, you see... and I know how to take care o' meself."

"I'm Irish, too," Mulcahy replied, "but that still doesn't explain your bruised knuckles."

"I did... not... kill... Mr. Murphy..." O'Brien said, now devolving into gut-wrenching sobs.

"I will give you one more chance," Mulcahy said, his foul breath once again assaulting the man's nostrils. After a few nauseating breaths, Mulcahy turned his back and left the room, switching off the lone bulb suspended from the ceiling. Nicholas O'Brien was now in total darkness.

Knowing when a man was at his lowest was an art form that Mulcahy had mastered early in his career as a police officer. Re-entering the room barely half an hour later,

Mulcahy turned on the light as O'Brien blinked his eyes open from a too-brief slumber. He was disoriented from both dehydration and sleep deprivation.

"One more chance, sunshine…" Mulcahy hissed, his eyes suddenly taking on an evil visage.

"I don't know…" Nicholas began.

Mulcahy snapped. Pivoting counterclockwise on the ball of his left foot, he roundhoused a closed-fisted blow to Nicholas's left eye socket. A scream of pain and disbelief followed.

"I am telling you the tru…" but the words did not entirely make it out of his mouth before a second punch came from the other direction. Another scream of pain as O'Brien struggled to remain conscious. The second blow was delivered with Mulcahy's full weight behind it.

O'Brien lolled in the chair and nearly toppled out of it before Mulcahy caught him and set him upright again. Once again, Mulcahy breathed into his face. "We know you did it, now tell us the truth."

At this point, all Nicholas could do was blubber incoherently. He was nearing his breaking point. Mulcahy knew from past interrogations that it would not be long before a confession followed. Once more, Mulcahy left the room – leaving the light on this time.

Fifteen minutes later, Mulcahy was back; this time, with a blackjack in his right hand that he slapped threateningly on his left palm. Nicholas O'Brien instantly recognized the weapon and knew a beating would follow. Scared and having been denied the opportunity to relieve himself since he was brought in, Nicholas uncontrollably voided his bladder.

"Piss all over my clean floor, will you?" Mulcahy bellowed. The admonishment was followed immediately by a blow of the blackjack to Nicholas's upper right arm. It was forceful enough to inflict severe pain, but not enough to cause permanent tissue damage.

"Mr. Murphy is dead. That's the only thing I know," O'Brien babbled. "I don't know how he got there or who killed him."

"We have a statement from one of the other factory workers that you were fired last week by Mr. Murphy. That gives you a reason to get revenge." Mulcahy accused. There was no such statement. Mulcahy had simply made it up.

"No, sir. Nobody was fired. Another Irishman got into an argument with Mr. Murphy. It was… it was… Seamus… Seamus Con…" O'Brien's sniveling was interrupted by a now-furious Mulcahy.

"Liar! You killed Murphy!" Mulcahy's next blow was intended for the soft tissue of the left deltoid muscle, a point where it would inflict severe pain and finally coerce a blubbering confession. Somehow, O'Brien sensed the blow was coming and flinched just enough so that Mulcahy's blackjack instead struck the occipital region of his skull. The force drove a fragment of the now-broken occipital bone forward, its trajectory severing his spinal cord. Death was instantaneous and Nicholas O'Brien's now-lifeless form slumped in the chair.

Mulcahy knew immediately what had happened. He had killed a man during an interrogation, one that was going nowhere. "Sergeant!" Mulcahy screamed in panic, "come here at once."

Sergeant Joseph Patterson entered the room and saw O'Brien's inert form slumped and hanging from his handcuffed left wrist. Without a word, he checked for a pulse and turned to look at Mulcahy. "He's dead. Call the City Coroner," Patterson ordered. "Mulcahy, to my office at once!" was his next order. Mulcahy complied without question; he respected his sergeant's authority.

For the next hour, Patterson grilled Mulcahy on the events in the interrogation room. Sean Mulcahy was resolute and consistent in his explanations, never deviating from his belief that Nicholas O'Brien was guilty of murder.

It didn't take Sergeant Patterson long to reach a decision. It would be in the best interests of the Baltimore City Police Department that Sean Mulcahy be dismissed, effective immediately. "Officer Mulcahy, to avoid embarrassment to the Baltimore Police Department, you are relieved of your police powers and no longer an officer of the law in this city. Please turn in your badge and gun."

Mulcahy knew that he had to comply with the Sergeant's directive. It was the way things were done in the early 20th Century when a police officer overstepped his authority. No fanfare. No public outcry. The officer just disappeared and no record other than "for personal reasons" was ever mentioned in his personnel file.

Dropping his badge and unloaded revolver on the Sergeant's desk, Mulcahy left the precinct for the last time. He was still in uniform, but without the accoutrements of power and authority. His fellow officers remained silent as he walked past them, especially the ones who observed that Mulcahy had been stripped of his badge. Those officers ceremoniously turned their back on Sean Mulcahy; he was no longer one of them and not worthy of their recognition nor respect.

Once outside the precinct, Mulcahy removed his police officer's tunic and threw it into a garbage bin. He now despised the uniform and what it had made him become.

Chapter Five: Motive and Opportunity
Pennsylvania, Beginning in 1902

After fleeing Baltimore, Seamus's life in domestic service to the Butler family had been tumultuous. He never felt like he fit in, and the constraints of decorum and deference wore on his normally industrious nature. Standing around waiting to be tasked by a person of supposedly superior social standing was not what he was cut out for. As time went on, Seamus bickered almost constantly with the senior members of the household staff and came dangerously close to being summarily dismissed on more than one occasion.

Bridgit, on the other hand, felt that she had moved up in the world from her days as a washerwoman at The Johns Hopkins Hospital. She quickly relaxed around Mrs. Florence Butler and her daughters, taking care of their every need from morning until night. Some nights, Bridgit was even allowed to accompany Mrs. Butler to cotillions and soirees around town, but always remained unobtrusively ready in the background with the rest of the servant cadre.

The dichotomy of the Conaty's existence wore on Seamus. After a while, he resented his wife's happy assimilation into servitude and swore that he would break away from that life as soon as he possibly could. It would be nearly three years before he came across Sparky Thompson and a suitable opportunity.

Working together with Bridgit at the Butler mansion in Allentown, Seamus was assigned to escort the Sparky as he electrified the residence. Without giving away his shipyard experience, Seamus made himself indispensable to Sparky. He held tools, he crawled in tight spaces to guide wires to their destination, he made sure Sparky had food to eat and water to drink.

"Seamus, get me one of the switches from the crate with the red marking," Sparky ordered one afternoon. "The red crate is where I keep the special switches and outlets for the homes of businessmen and their families,"

By the end of the week, Seamus was clamoring for Sparky to take him on as an apprentice. It didn't take Sparky long to decide, as he had just signed a contract to electrify one of Allentown's mills, owned by Waldo Emerson Butler. Sparky needed more help, so it was only logical to take Seamus on as an apprentice.

Seamus quickly resigned from his position in the Butler household after Sparky made his offer. Before resigning, Seamus had installed an electrical switch in the bedroom occupied by Edgar Allan Butler, the eldest son of Waldo and Florence Butler. Seamus had intended to use what he had learned at the Harland-Wolff shipyard and modify the switch so that it would cause problems later – but when he examined the switch, the modification had already been done. What Seamus didn't realize was that the supposed modification was actually a manufacturing defect in the switch.

Seamus wanted revenge on the entire household which had, in his mind, treated him so badly. He knew that the Butlers relied on the domestic staff for even the smallest task, including operating the new light switches. The modification to the switch controlling the light in Edgar's bedroom was certain to shock *someone*. It was just a matter of time until that happened; and Seamus didn't care if it was a member of the Butler family or one of the domestic staff.

Once the Butler mansion was complete, Sparky began his contract with Waldo Emerson Butler to bring electric lighting into the mill. It would be a costly job, Sparky explained, but the added lighting meant that the crews could begin working around the clock. Butler instantly recognized that this could double or even triple the mill's output – and his profits.

The work in the mill went quickly, as they were installing wiring across wide expanses of open areas and not snaking wires through walls, except to reach the offices of the factory management. For the offices, Sparky once again installed switches and outlets from the red crate.

Both Sparky and Seamus engaged in polite conversation with the laborers as they went about their tasks. The electricians observed that, for the most part, the mill men were disgruntled with their lot in life, knowing that there was little they could do to change it.

The mill workers needed more money and less reliance on the so-called "company store" for their necessities and housing. Sometimes, the men were even paid in scrip instead of currency, with the scrip being valid only in the company store. They lived from payday to payday.

Unionization was the only real answer to their plight, and Sparky vowed to help make that happen. To that end, he quietly gave a portion of his cash – paid to him by the mill's owner, Waldo Emerson Butler -- to union organizers within the Butler mill complex. It was risky: if Sparky were to be discovered funding the unionization effort, he would never work for the rich and powerful of Allentown again.

Sparky's donations were always in small amounts and always in cash. Ten dollars here, five dollars there. Never large sums at once. The union organizers certainly appreciated it and allowing the coffers to grow over time was definitely in their best interests.

Knowing that their work was about finished, Seamus began packing up their tools and remaining hardware. As he gathered the crates and canvas bags to the front entrance of the mill to load in their wagon, he noticed a familiar figure. The man turned towards Seamus and as he did, a scar across the left side of his face became visible.

Seamus nearly dropped the crate he was carrying, and he fought to retain his composure. It was the police officer he ran into after the incident in Baltimore. Seamus's heart raced. Why was *that* man here? Would he be recognized? Was he a suspect? Seamus kept his head low so that the scarred man would not see his face.

It was only a couple of minutes before Mr. Butler bellowed from his office, "Mr. Mulcahy, please come in!" A sudden breeze through the mill flapped Mulcahy's unbuttoned jacket open and Seamus could clearly see a pearl handled pistol in a shoulder holster under Mulcahy's left arm.

Waldo Emerson Butler's *basso profundo* voice resonated enough that Seamus could hear parts of the conversation that was taking place inside the private office. It was clear that Mulcahy was no longer a police officer and instead was Butler's henchman. That, in Seamus's opinion, made him even more dangerous as he would surely be aware of ways to circumvent the law with the support of the rich and powerful Butler.

"Make it end," Butler told Mulcahy. "I don't care how you do it, just do what needs to be done," slamming the table with his fist for emphasis.

"Yes, sir," was Mulcahy's reply.

"Sparky, we need to get out of here... fast!" Seamus blurted out after Mulcahy was inside Butler's office and beyond earshot. "That man who just arrived... I saw him in Baltimore. Well... more like ran into him. He was a copper back then. I recognize the scar on his face and the eyes that showed no feeling."

"He's done nothing to you, Seamus," Sparky replied. "He could be a good man. I don't know if Mr. Butler would have a bad man, one with a past, on his payroll."

"Even good men can go bad," Seamus countered. "Please, Sparky, can we move along now?" Seamus's voice trembled as he spoke.

"Yes. We can go back to the hotel and get changed for dinner," Sparky responded cheerily. "We will leave town the day after tomorrow and head to Harrisburg."

"We can't leave soon enough," Seamus said.

The rest of the evening was uneventful. They had a sumptuous dinner to celebrate the end of a grueling job: steak cooked medium rare, baked potatoes, sauteed onions, green beans, and a bottle of cabernet sauvignon, vintage 1895. It was a feast for kings. Sparky and Seamus were, for that moment, on top of their world. Over a snifter of brandy and a fine cigar after dinner, Sparky asked Seamus, "Where should we go next?" The discussion of their options continued well into the night.

The next morning, Sparky settled their account at the hotel. After paying Seamus's wages and taking a cut for himself, there was still enough money left for a hefty donation to the union organizers. Because they were leaving Allentown, Sparky felt no trepidation for leaving a lump-sum cash donation behind as long as the organizers listed it in their records as an "anonymous benefactor."

Chapter Six: Go West, Young Man!
On to Harrisburg, late 1906

The departure from Allentown was hastened by Seamus's unsettling encounter with Sean Mulcahy. The next logical city to temporarily call home was Harrisburg, as they had agreed the night before. Not only was it the state capital, but it was also a major hub for the Pennsylvania Railroad.

When they reached Harrisburg, Sparky and Seamus took a temporary room at a boarding house in the Allison Hill suburb and focused their energy on the Mount Pleasant section where the wealthier citizens lived in their Colonial Revivalist homes. Word of Sparky's skills quickly spread, and Archibald Thompson was soon in the employ of a rail and steel magnate, Isaiah Henry Frankel, to electrify a summer home on a somewhat distant hill overlooking the city.

On his first visit to the Frankel summer home, Sparky surveyed the structure for the outlet, switching, and light fixture requirements. He quickly composed a list that he telegrammed to his friend, John Garfield, back in New Jersey. A return telegram acknowledged receipt and indicated that the requested hardware would be arriving as soon as the U.S. Mail could deliver it.

The Frankel summer home's layout was more complex than most, so it took Sparky longer than usual to bring electricity to every room. Mr. Frankel insisted that the servants' quarters be wired as well. He wanted his servants to be happy, even when they were away from the main house in town. "They were, after all, entitled to some leisure time at the summer home," Frankel was fond of saying. It didn't matter to him that they were on call twenty-four hours a day and likely would not engage in any leisure pursuit other than sleeping or bedtime reading.

Sparky took extra care with planning the wiring of the servants' quarters. He felt they were entitled to the same quality service as the rest of the Frankel homes. Electricity, Sparky knew, was the way of the future and he could envision many labor-saving devices that would make the plight of those in service easier.

At the Frankel summer home, the servants were generally housed two to a room, except for the major-domo and head housekeeper, who had their own rooms which doubled as offices. The other eight servants, four of each gender, were responsible for the care of the lady of the house and the children around the clock. The rest of the servants, including a chauffeur, always remained behind at the mansion in town to care for Mr. Frankel and sometimes his mistress, who would visit when Mrs. Adelaide Frankel and the children were away.

The Frankel children, Henry, William, and Henrietta were all in their teens when Sparky wired the summer home. Every one of them lorded their station in life over everyone around them and treated the servants with contempt. Sparky and Seamus were no different. They may not have been servants, but the Frankel children treated them as such. Both of the men bristled with irritation whenever the Frankel children ordered them around.

"Anne, get me my bathrobe," Adelaide Frankel would demand as she stepped out of the bath. "… and a towel, too. I need drying off." The unsaid message was that Adelaide was expecting Anne to dry off her body. No "please," no "thank you," just a condescending instruction.

Henrietta, barely fifteen years old, was no less demanding than her mother. Still developing into womanhood and slightly overweight, Henrietta was prone to mood swings and would lash out at the servants whenever she felt slighted by their behavior.

"Rebecca!" Henrietta shouted one afternoon. "I want a sandwich… *now*!"

Poor Rebecca could only do what she had been trained to do. She would run to the kitchen and put together a crustless sandwich for "Miss Henrietta," usually with meat left over from the night before. Most of the time, the meat would not be to Henrietta's liking and would end up either being thrown across the room or fed unceremoniously to one of the many dogs that had free run of the summer house. "I hate this stuff… whatever it is…" Henrietta would wail, never mind that she had eaten several servings of it the night before.

"That little bitch," Rebecca would grumble under her breath whenever Henrietta became insufferable. "I deserve better than this," she would think. "I get treated – and fed – worse than the family dogs."

Henry, the eldest of the children at eighteen, was no better. Isaiah Frankel had been teaching his son the ways of business during the school year but insisted that Henry spend his last season at the summer home before going abroad to explore the sights of Europe. More of a petulant child than an adult, Henry was even more demanding and condescending than his sister.

The youngest, William, was still a boy soprano in the church choir. A timid sort, William rarely spoke to anyone but his mother except to voice disapproval when things didn't go his way. If his demands weren't met, it was likely that a temper tantrum would follow, and Adelaide would berate whatever servant was nearest for their lack of attention.

Sparky and Seamus observed all of this behavior while they were working in the family quarters on the second floor. Try as they might, the occasional tirade from the Frankel children was unavoidable. The one thing Sparky had in his favor was that he could excuse himself to be elsewhere in the house to fetch tools or materials. Invariably, it was Seamus who bore the brunt of their harangues.

Mr. Frankel often visited the home on summer weekends. While he was there, the children were always on their best behavior and Adelaide was the model wife, submissive to her husband's whims and control. Anything Isaiah Frankel wanted, Isaiah Frankel got, including some rather unusual predilections in the marital bedroom. Adelaide tolerated them, all the while knowing he had already shared the experiences with his secretary-mistress in town and was just using her as a continuum of his erotic deviances.

The Frankel family was, in Sparky's opinion, broken. Perhaps broken beyond repair. They had so much money and power it was almost obscene. "Something needs to be done," Sparky commiserated with Seamus over a beer at the local tavern. "That family needs to be put back in its place," he would grumble.

About three weeks after Sparky began work on the Frankel summer home, the job was complete. First, he took the major-domo and head housekeeper around the home to show them how everything worked. He pointed out where all the switches were located. Next, he explained where outlets were located for the plug-in lamps that were replacing gas lamps or kerosene lanterns. Only the largest rooms such as the front parlor had more than one outlet.

After Sparky was satisfied the domestic staff knew where everything was and how it operated, he dismissed Seamus and gave less detailed instructions to Adelaide Frankel and the children, as he knew it was unlikely they would be doing any switching on or off on their own. Sparky also emphasized safety around electricity and made sure the Frankels knew that electricity and water were not a good combination.

"Master Frankel," Sparky said as he was showing Henry the lights in his bedroom, "I have seen what happens to men who are sent to the electric chair." Sparky had never seen an execution in person, but he had read accounts of them in the newspapers. Besides being an electrician, Archibald Thompson was also an engaging and convincing story-teller.

"It's supposed to be quick and painless... I can read the newspapers," Henry Frankel retorted. "One flip of a switch, and 'zap!' it's done." Henry pushed the switch buttons on and off several times for emphasis.

"It's not quite that glamorous, Master Frankel. First the man is strapped to the chair at the chest, wrists, and ankles. He's already had a monk's tonsure shaven into his head before he gets to the chair. Then a wet sponge is placed on his newly-shorn head and a metal cap is placed over that, then strapped under his chin."

Henry Frankel's eyes were wide with amazement. He hardly knew this man... this person only slightly better than a servant... and here he was describing how a man died from electricity. Describing the execution with exceptional detail. It made Henry squirm.

Sparky continued, "Once the metal cap is placed on his head, each foot is put in a shallow metal pan with just enough warm water to cover his feet." Sparky paused for effect. "The warm water usually makes the man lose control of his own water and a yellow puddle forms under his chair."

"Mr. Thompson... Sparky... you need to stop now. You're scaring me..." Henry said, his voice wavering in fear and its tone no longer condescending.

"Son, you need to hear this..." Sparky said firmly. "After that, the warden waits until the appointed hour in deference to the possibility of the governor calling with a stay of execution. They wait another five minutes for good measure, usually with the convict groveling for mercy and peeing his pants."

"Enough, Mr. Thompson... I've heard enough..." Henry cried as he started to panic.

Sparky would not be deterred. "When those five minutes are up, the executioners throw a large switch in another room. They are out of sight of the execution chamber. That switch powers up the transformers that will deliver the lethal shock." Another long pause for effect. "In another room, once the voltmeter reaches the required voltage, three other men throw switches at the same time; their assignments were drawn by lot. None of them knows which one was wired to the chair."

"With the flip of that switch," Sparky clapped his hands together loudly, which made Henry jump, "the man receives a jolt like a thousand lightning bolts and in less than thirty seconds, he is dead… I will spare you the details of what happens to his body when the electric current passes through. It's enough to say that it isn't a pretty sight… so… *please* be careful with the electricity in this house and *never* allow water and electricity within a yard of each other."

Henry's face went pale and the smell of urine was pervasive. He had not wet himself since before puberty and here was this hired man scaring him half to death. At this point, Henry was speechless from the fear. He would have nightmares for several nights following Sparky's graphic explanation.

The story finished, Sparky turned on his heels, strode out of Henry's bedroom, and was out the front door without so much as a "goodbye." Gathering Seamus, their tools, and supplies, they headed back to the rooming house and began a discussion of where to head next.

The next morning, Sparky left Seamus behind and went to the Frankel home in town to collect his fees. As with the Butler home, Sparky had significantly inflated the material costs, claiming that everything he used was "premium grade." Isaiah Frankel wrote a check for the artificially escalated amount without question.

Sparky went to the local bank to cash the check. He had no problem doing so, once the clerk saw who had written the check: Isaiah Henry Frankel, the richest man in Harrisburg.

"Mr. Thompson, in what denominations would you like your cash?" the clerk asked politely.

Sparky replied, "it doesn't matter as long as it is real money…"

With seven hundred and fifty dollars in hand, Archibald Thompson and Seamus Conaty were on their way to Pittsburgh. It was December 2, 1906.

Chapter Seven: Obituary
Back in Allentown, 1906

THE MORNING CALL

Allentown, Pennsylvania – December 8, 1906

SON OF WEALTHY MILL OWNER DEAD

Edgar Allan Butler, twenty-one-year-old son of mill owner Waldo Emerson Butler, perished at home on Sunday evening. The cause of death is believed to be electrocution.

Just before sunrise on Sunday morning, the Butler's housekeeper, Mrs. Helen Finch, found the young Mr. Butler unconscious in the doorway to his bedroom. The family sent immediately for their physician, Dr. Robert Mittford, who pronounced young Mr. Butler dead at the scene.

A preliminary evaluation by Dr. Mittford suggested that Butler was shocked by an electric light switch just outside the doorway to his private bath. According to the good doctor, there were burn marks on Butler's index finger and opposite heel, consistent with the path an electric charge would have taken through his body. The body was removed to the County Coroner's Office for further examination and possible autopsy.

Edgar Allan Butler is survived by his parents, Waldo Emerson Butler and Florence Elizabeth (nee Southwick) Butler. Also surviving are his unmarried twin sister, Louisa May, and unmarried younger sisters Agnes Ida and Myrtle Grace, all are still living at home in the care of their parents.

Funeral arrangements are not yet complete, and the Butler home is in a state of mourning. The family wishes not to be disturbed during this difficult time and will make an announcement in this paper when funeral arrangements are complete.

*　*　*　*　*

What the newspaper article did not say, out of deference to common decency, was that Edgar Allan Butler was naked and only partially covered by a thick towel, which, it was later revealed, was placed by Mrs. Finch to maintain what little dignity Edgar had left. It was obvious that he had just come from a bath; the scents of hibiscus and lavender were almost overpowering.

Edgar Allen Butler had fallen down on his left side, with his left arm extended towards and partially up the wall below the light switch. He had also experienced a "death

viii

erection," which Mittford had read about in medical journal articles about violent death. The articles said that such a phenomenon, known as priapism in medical parlance, was not uncommon – but usually accompanied more traumatic deaths such as hanging or gunshot wounds. The journals, however, did not note whether post-mortem priapism had been observed following executions by electric chair.

Doctor Mittford was puzzled by the unexpected and seemingly accidental death of one of Allentown's up-and-coming young men. Electricity was relatively new in town, but Mittford knew that its safety far exceeded that of old-fashioned gaslights or kerosene lanterns. He had followed the number of fire brigade responses since electrification and had already concluded that Allentown was a safer place because of electricity: deaths from asphyxiation and fire had been dramatically reduced.

Mittford, having been the Butler family physician since before the Butler twins were born, also knew that Edgar Allan Butler was healthy as a horse; therefore, he expected no unusual findings in the coroner's report. Butler was a non-drinker, only smoked an occasional cigar in social situations, and exercised regularly. Mittford did find it strange that such a virile, eligible, and *rich* young man never had a line of potential female romantic interests outside his door.

After a few days, the County Coroner provided his report to Dr. Mittford. The cause of death was confirmed to be electrocution, as Mittford first declared, but the coroner also determined the death to be accidental. Doctor Mittford was not convinced and suspected foul play.

"Who could have had access to the bathroom and set a scheme in motion?" Mittford thought to himself. "Could someone have tampered with the switch, making it dangerous?"

Mittford was in a quandary. Should he challenge the County Coroner and force an inquest, or should he accept the finding of "accidental death by electrocution," one that would have ensured a quick settlement from the Butler's double-indemnity life insurance policies? A full-blown investigation could, in the worst case, produce evidence prejudicial to the original finding and negate the double indemnity clause of Butler's insurance policy.

After a nearly sleepless night, Dr. Mittford decided he had to meet with Waldo Butler. He felt duty-bound to inform Butler of his suspicions, even if it meant losing the entire family as patients. Complicating Mittford's dilemma was knowledge that the County Coroner would not have been elected to his position without financial support from the Butler coffers. He suspected that the County Coroner would produce whatever finding suited the needs of Waldo Emerson Butler.

Mittford called Butler on the telephone the next morning. Working through Butler's secretary (widely known to be his mistress as well), a noon luncheon appointment was set. They would meet at the gentlemen's club in town where both were members. Dr. Mittford also arranged for his routine patient appointments to be rescheduled. He did not want to run the risk of being late or missing the luncheon entirely.

The conversation between the two men, conducted in the privacy of a quiet corner endowed with overstuffed leather furniture popular at the time, was strained. Waldo Emerson Butler, though he had just lost an adult child, seemed only to be worried about the bottom line, the payout from the insurance company. Dr. Robert Mittford, on the other hand, wanted to be sure that the death was not willfully or maliciously caused. Mittford thought he was looking out for his friend's interests.

The two men eventually moved to a private table to partake of their mid-day meal. Smoked salmon, fresh from the icebox, was first, followed by a bouillabaisse laden with crabmeat from the Chesapeake Bay. The main course was roast canvasback duck from the Susquehanna flats, with seared potatoes and root vegetables.

"With your permission, Waldo, I would like to turn this matter over to our constabulary in hopes that they will bring in experts from Pittsburgh or Philadelphia," Mittford explained. "I don't see how your son's death was completely accidental. There have only been a handful of electrocution deaths in Pennsylvania and neighboring states since electrification began some twenty years ago."

Waldo Emerson Butler tented his fingers below his chin. He was deep in mental calculations of what effect a finding of anything other than accidental death would have on the money. It was money he desperately needed to finance some much-needed capital improvements to the mill.

"Robert, I trust the coroner's report that my son's death was accidental. I hope that you will see your way clear of your deductions that it was caused by anything to the contrary," Butler patronized. He was, without directly suggesting it, that Mittford drop his interest in the cause of death.

Dr. Mittford was speechless and puzzled. He had known Waldo Emerson Butler for over three decades. This was the first inkling of any shift in Butler's mindset that favored money over family. Was Butler in trouble so deep that he needed the double indemnity pay-out from the life insurance policy? Mittford decided that the circumstances were not ideal for him to press the issue. They barely spoke for the remainder of the meal.

*   *   *   *   *

After a postprandial cigar and the departure of Dr Mittford, Butler motioned for his private detective, who had been unobtrusively seated in the shadows of the dining room, to come to his table. The detective, Sean Mulcahy, took a seat at Butler's table that was always within visual contact with as many points of entry as possible. He had learned long ago that constant vigilance was essential to survival, and his chosen seat reflected that knowledge. His eyes never stopped scanning the room for threats.

Mulcahy was a beast of a man. Overweight, but in a way that reflected physical strength rather than corpulence, it was obvious that he could and would protect Butler from any and all threats. He was always armed and the bulge of a pearl-handled handgun in a cross-draw holster under his left arm was not very well hidden by his suitcoat.

A few years earlier, Mulcahy had been discharged from the Baltimore Police Department for beating a murder suspect to death during an interrogation. Though charges were never filed, it was the end of Mulcahy's law enforcement career. His red hair and neatly-trimmed beard added to his fearsome visage. A jagged scar, left behind by a poorly healed knife wound, arched from his left nostril to left ear and added an aura that left most rational men cowering in their boots.

It was ironic that Mulcahy was employed by Waldo Emerson Butler. An Irishman, Mulcahy's grandfather had been killed in a horrific accident during construction of the Transcontinental Railroad along with over 100 other roustabouts when a premature detonation of explosive charges caused a massive landslide. At times, Mulcahy wanted revenge for his grandfather's death, which he believed was indirectly caused by the indifference of rich railroad tycoons to the plight of their workforce. After being released from the Baltimore Police Department, Mulcahy needed work and private security seemed to be a natural extension of his experiences; Butler was merely a source of income for the former police officer.

Butler leaned into the conversation, speaking in hushed tones, "Sean, I need you to make sure that the real reason my son died never comes to light. Whatever it takes… whatever it costs… that quack Mittford needs to be put off the chase. One wrong move and I will be financially ruined. I need that insurance money if I am to stay afloat financially." Butler was certain that no one else in the club could hear their conversation; the closest occupied table was a good twenty feet away. The din of the dining room and a member plinking away obnoxiously on the grand piano drowned out the chance of being overheard.

"Aye, sir. I understand," Mulcahy replied as he stood up to leave. "If he gets too close, I will take matters… well… it's best if I don't share the details with you, Mr. Butler."

As fluidly as he arrived at Butler's private table, Mulcahy skulked silently and unceremoniously out the back door of the club. He was on a mission. The first thing he had to do was to get his hands on the County Coroner's Report.

Butler, too, left the club – but did not return directly to his office. He dropped in on his attorney, Abner Whipple.

Whipple was on retainer to both the Butler businesses and to the Butler family. The position was financially lucrative for Whipple, who spent little on the trappings of his profession: his office was a mishmash of old papers and journals; he had no clerks nor secretarial staff; and his office was lit by a single incandescent electric light bulb. His residence was above the office and was just as spartan and still had not been hooked up to the building's nascent electrical service. The only thing that indicated his building housed a law practice was a well-weathered sign outside the front door:

ABNER WHIPPLE, ESQ.
ATTORNEY AT LAW

Closing the door behind him and making sure that he had not been followed, Butler plopped down in the rickety chair in front of Whipple's desk. The chair groaned under the weight of Butler's massive frame.

"Mr. Butler, what can I do for you today?" Whipple asked, his voice shrill and whiny.

"As you know, my son was recently killed... electrocuted... in his own bedroom," Butler explained. "When Edgar was born twenty-one years ago, I took out a life insurance policy on him – but not his twin sister – with a double indemnity clause in case of an accidental death."

"I see no problem with that payout happening," Whipple replied. "I have read the policy and it is iron-clad."

"You've told me that many times," Butler said, the irritation in his voice rising. "But new information has come to light that could put the payout in jeopardy. What I am about to tell you is to stay between us. You are my attorney."

"Of course. You should not worry otherwise," Whipple asserted.

"Doctor Mittford suspects that Edgar's death was anything other than accidental. He knows that I financed the County Coroner's election and, as such, Mittford might think the Coroner has been paid off to have the cause of death determination go my way," Butler explained.

"According to Pennsylvania law, the Coroner's findings can only be challenged through a formal inquest. We would have to bring outside experts to Allentown and have them examine all aspects of your son's death. We really do not want that to happen," said Whipple.

"I also have to tell you, as my attorney, that the mill is in financial trouble. I invested all of its working capital in Union Pacific Railroad stock. It has lost fifty percent of its value since September. I need that life insurance payout to keep my business solvent," Butler railed.

Whipple pursed his lips as he thought. He exhaled heavily through his nose before telling Butler, "There has to be a way to protect your claim, legal or otherwise."

"Make it quick, Whipple," Butler commanded. "The insurance company is starting to sniff around for the Coroner's records, and if they get to Doc Mittford, my goose is cooked."

Butler rose, pushing his chair noisily back, and glared at Whipple to emphasize his point. He then turned and strode purposefully out the door. Whipple had every reason to fear Waldo Emerson Butler: if it weren't for Butler, Whipple would never have been admitted before the Pennsylvania Bar.

*   *   *   *   *

The next morning, Doctor Mittford entered his practice to prepare for his day of seeing patients. He was a man of routine. First, he stopped by the receptionist's desk and was greeted cheerily by Mrs. Hanscomb, who had worked for Mittford for as long as he had been in Allentown. Going over her notes, Mittford saw that his schedule for the day included house calls to several heavily pregnant women who, because of their social standing, would not allow themselves to be seen in public in their current condition.

"Thank you, Mrs. Hanscomb, for being thorough as always. I shall be in my office for the next hour, studying."

"Yes, Doctor. I will make sure you are not disturbed," Mrs. Hanscomb replied.

Mittford had the only key to his private office, a space that not even his most trusted friend, Mrs. Hanscomb, could access. When he opened the door and turned on the overhead light, Mittford was met by the smell of garlic and onions, thinking that he might have forgotten to empty the waste bin the night before. It was then that he saw a shadowy figure seated behind his desk and facing the bookshelves on the back wall.

Slowly, the figure turned; Mittford instantly recognized the visage of Sean Mulcahy, Waldo Emerson Butler's private detective, who Mittford thought was more of a henchman than investigator. As the chair swiveled around even further, Mulcahy began rolling a .45 caliber shell casing back and forth between his hands – while at the same time letting his ill-fitting suitcoat fall open to reveal a pearl-handled pistol slung menacingly in a shoulder holster.

"Mr. Mulcahy, what can I do for you this morning?" Mittford asked, trying to keep the panic out of his voice.

"I am sure you know who my boss is, Doctor Mittford." Mulcahy paused for effect. "He has asked me to convey a message to you, that you should tread lightly in your dealings with the County Coroner in regard to the death of my employer's eldest son." Mulcahy was choosing his words carefully so that he would not mention his boss by name. "In fact, Doctor Mittford, it would be in your best interests to leave the case alone entirely."

The silence that followed was deafening. Mulcahy broke the silence by drawing his weapon from its holster, ejecting the clip, and inserting the round into magazine. For emphasis, Mulcahy slammed the clip back into the base of the grip and slid the action back-and-forth to chamber the round. Mittford flinched with each metallic sound and it was all he could do to retain control of his bladder and bowels. He knew Mulcahy was threatening him and had little doubt that this odiferous monster of a man was quite capable of making good on that threat.

Chapter Eight: A Slight Detour
Chambersburg, Pennsylvania

Archibald Thompson and Seamus Conaty boarded a train for Pittsburgh once their work at the Frankel home was complete. The Cumberland Valley Railroad line took the easiest path through the mountains, first going slightly south through Chambersburg. A twist of fate and a disabling breakdown of a locomotive left Thompson and Conaty stranded there, potentially for several days.

Chambersburg seemed to be an opportunity just waiting for the two electricians to arrive. Electricity had just reached the town, supplied from a coal-fired generator near Hagerstown, Maryland. When Sparky and Seamus arrived, barely ten percent of the businesses along Main Street had been at least partially electrified, and residential service was still lacking.

John Thomas Chalmers – "J. T." to his friends – was among the richest men in town. Not known for his philanthropy, he lorded his riches over the rest of the citizens. A shrewd lumber merchant, he was a partner in an enterprise that sold the lumber to rebuild the town after it was burned by Confederate soldiers in 1864. The people of

Chambersburg tolerated him because of his free-spending ways. What Chalmers wanted, Chalmers got. It was as simple as that.

The one thing J. T. Chalmers lacked was electricity. There was service to Philadelphia Avenue for sure, but it went straight to Wilson College on the other side of the street. None of the homes had yet been hooked up.

Chalmers knew that once he had electricity, the other homeowners would want it, too. He smelled another money-making opportunity, as the other residents of Philadelphia Avenue were very competitive and would just have to have the latest in modern electric conveniences. Somehow, he would capitalize on the perceived demand. He just wasn't sure how.

Meanwhile, Sparky and Seamus had checked into a rooming house on a back alley near the Old Jail once they had decided to stay. Sharing a room was half as expensive as separate accommodations. Their space, however, was reduced considerably when they moved all the tools of their trade into the room. Sparky was adamant that their equipment, especially the switches and outlets in the red-marked crate, never be left anywhere other than their room or job site.

With Sparky paying their way out of their earnings from Harrisburg, Seamus could not complain: it wasn't *his* money that was being spent, except for beers at the local tavern. For more-or-less free room and board, Seamus could tolerate almost anything.

Chalmers, despite his wealth and membership in the town's exclusive gentlemen's club, preferred taking his mid-day meals and his drink in the seedier establishments in Chambersburg. "Lunch," Chalmers often pontificated, "was the working man's time. Dinner, on the other hand, was a more formal repast and the attire should be appropriate." It was pure coincidence that he was seated near Sparky and Seamus one afternoon and overheard most of their conversation.

"Seamus, I tell you we have an opportunity here. A gold mine. Not much of this town has been wired for electricity yet, and we're the men to do it. We did well in Harrisburg and Allentown. Too well, almost... that check that Mr. Frankel gave us will keep us in food and drink for several weeks," Sparky said, barely able to contain his excitement.

"Aye, 'tis a good thing to be busy, sure enough," Seamus replied, slipping into a clipped Irish brogue that surfaced whenever he had been drinking a little more than he should have. "I can send me money home t'ma missus as long as yer willin' t' keep me on."

Their conversation was interrupted by a man clearing his throat, not out of need but to get their attention. Sparky and Seamus looked up from their meal of boiled beef and potatoes and made eye contact with Chalmers. Seamus had been sipping his beer and abruptly pulled the mug away from his mouth as Chalmers spoke, leaving a foam moustache behind.

"Gentlemen, I am John Chalmers and I own a rather large home on Philadelphia Avenue." He stopped short of calling it a mansion; that would have been pretentious, he thought to himself. "I am in the market for my home to be wired for electricity and I could not help but overhear that you had done some work for a Mr. Frankel in Harrisburg. That wouldn't be Isaiah Frankel, would it?"

"The very same," Sparky replied. "We wired his summer home this past season. I am Archibald Thompson… my friends call me 'Sparky.' This fine gentleman to my left is Mr. Seamus Conaty. He's from Ireland and is my apprentice."

"I know Frankel by name and by reputation but have never met the man. I've heard he doesn't pay for anything that would not benefit him in the long run and certainly doesn't suffer fools. Whatever he paid you to wire up his vacation home, I will pay you double," Chalmers said conspiratorially.

"Mr. Chalmers," Sparky said, recognizing an opportunity, "Mr. Frankel paid us... fifteen hundred dollars... plus materials." Sparky had set the trap. If Chalmers took the bait, they would have more money in hand than most labor union men made in four years.

"I accept your terms, Mr. Thompson. I ask that you start work on Monday. If there is anything you need, you can have it put on my account at the hardware store on Cleveland Avenue. Just tell the owner, Jacob Hausmann, that I sent you. If he asks for my wife's name, it is Mary. Mary Elizabeth Chalmers. Can you remember that?"

"Of course, Mr. Chalmers. Monday it is. Mary is a wonderful name, my own mother's as a matter of fact," Sparky replied. His mother's name was really Abigail, but Chalmers had no way of checking. Sparky was becoming a very adept salesman. He had already figured Chalmers out as a free spender who had no regard for the true cost of things, except for his cheap lunchtime meals and watery beer in working men's taverns.

"My home is the one with the red turret and tan window trim. You can't miss it," Chalmers explained. "There's one more thing, gentlemen…" he said as he leaned in and lowered his voice to just above a whisper, "the fee I am paying you is not to be discussed with anyone else, not even my wife. I shall trust your discretion in this matter."

Sparky and Seamus had Friday and the entire weekend to prepare for their next job, bilking John Thomas Chalmers out of over a thousand dollars of his money. With the Chalmers job under their belts, the remainder of Chambersburg society was sure to follow his example. With the added benefit of a handshake agreement not to discuss Chalmers's payment, Sparky could charge whatever he wanted to with impunity.

Sparky spent Friday and Saturday getting the materials he needed to connect the Chalmers house to the electrical service. The main line was across the street and it would be an easy task for the two men to connect a branch line to the Chalmers house. They could run the wire on Monday and get the necessary approval from the municipal authority on Tuesday. After those two details were complete, it would be a relatively simple task to electrify the Chalmers home.

"Seamus, I won't need you until Monday morning, so if you want to go back to Allentown on the train and spend the weekend with your darling wife, I am all for it. A man pining for his wife can be distracted and working with electricity requires his full attention," Sparky explained.

"Yes, boss. I think I would like to catch the evening train," Seamus replied. "I haven't seen Bridgit in over a month..." Excusing himself, he returned to the rooming house, packed a small travel duffel, and was on his way to the train station. Sparky never could understand what kept men like Seamus rushing home to their wives – or to brothel – at every opportunity. The only woman in his life would always be his mother; he had no room for emotional entanglement with anyone else.

While he was assembling the necessary supplies and equipment, Sparky realized just how revered the Chalmers name was in Chambersburg. All he had to do was say "I'm working on a job for Mr. Chalmers," and doors opened for him. Credit was arranged. Deliveries were expedited, with suppliers receiving telegrams for orders. Sparky thought to himself that he could get used to this sort of groveling in a hurry.

Seamus returned to the rooming house on Sunday evening, smelling of sweat and a woman's perfume, a scent which Sparky recognized from someplace, but couldn't remember where. He wondered if his apprentice had managed to spend private time with his wife or if he had instead sought the comforts of a woman in one of the seedier areas of Allentown. It was too much to worry about with such a large and lucrative job looming before them.

"Seamus, so glad that you are back in plenty of time to be rested before we start work in the morning. You'll need your rest. Get some sleep if you can," Sparky instructed; his own mind, however, was racing and he was unable to relax. He played the discussion with Mr. Chalmers over and over again in his head, trying to justify the amount he would be charging for such a simple task.

Mornings at the rooming house were becoming routine for Sparky and Seamus. The aroma of fresh bacon and fried potatoes wafting upstairs always managed to awaken Sparky: in his childhood, fresh bacon was a treat, usually only after a relative or friend butchered a hog. Those pleasant memories always seemed to flood Sparky's subconscious just before he was fully awake.

The two electricians looked forward to the banter around the table with the other residents, the strong black coffee, and the delectable food, always served family style. They certainly did not want for more food when they left for a hard day's work. The fried eggs, cured bacon or ham, homemade biscuits, gravy, potatoes, and coffee kept them satisfied until lunch time.

Breakfast complete, Sparky and Seamus headed for Philadelphia Avenue. Before entering the Chalmers property, they surveyed the existing service line across the street and found a conveniently placed transformer. Based on its size, despite providing service to nearby Wilson College, it had excess capacity that could power several homes on Philadelphia Avenue "and the rest of the college," Sparky mused. It might be a later opportunity he could exploit.

Meeting with Mr. Chalmers before starting work, Sparky made his needs known.

"Mr. Chalmers, portions of the college are already electrified. If we could tap into their transformer station, it would save considerable material costs," Sparky explained. "Otherwise, we will have to get the local authorities to approve running a line up from the south on this side of the street– and I would expect your neighbors would want access to it as well."

Chalmers immediately understood the economics of what Sparky was explaining. It would be necessary to reach out to the college and get their permission to access the transformer. It took less than an hour for Chalmers to exert his influence on the college's president, who approved the request without so much as losing a breath. Chalmers also envisioned the potential for making money off his neighbors' desire for electrical service; using the college's transformer had just saved him a significant amount of money.

Sparky recognized that it really would be best to dead-wire the Chalmers home first and then connect it to the live service. It was safer that way, with no live wires to contend with as they routed the cabling through a knob-and-tube system, starting below grade in the cellar, then working to the upper floors. Snaking the wires through the walls was relatively easy but cutting into the walls themselves to place switches and receptacles was tedious, painstaking work with a brace and bit, hammer, and chisel. The baseboards were hand-tooled oak planks and the walls were a combination of oyster shell plaster and spruce lath.

By the end of the week, Sparky and Seamus had completed all of the terminal wiring for the Chalmers home. They made provisions for electric lights and receptacles in every room, including the meager servants' quarters at the rear and in the attic of the structure. It was now time to hook the house up to the transformer across the street.

As their work progressed, Sparky reiterated that the hardware from the red crate was only to be used in the family quarters and never in the servants' spaces. Seamus furrowed his brow as he tried to understand the difference between the two. The hardware appeared identical: the switches had mother-of-pearl inlays on the buttons and the outlets were all made of a black ceramic. Seamus finally decided that it was not worth pressing for an explanation.

At the end of the week, Sparky and Seamus were on the front porch assembling their tools and parts to load their hand-drawn wagon for their return to the rooming house. Chalmers, who had suddenly appeared on the porch without making a sound, wanted a status report; he was becoming impatient that the work was taking so long.

"Mr. Thompson, a word, please?" Chalmers grumbled as he beckoned Sparky inside.

Stepping inside the massive front door, Sparky gave Chalmers a report. "Mr. Chalmers, we are done with the actual wiring of your wonderful home. I think it would be best, though, if we were to wait until Monday to connect the live service line. We've been working hard all week, ten hours a day, often in cramped quarters. Being tired is no way to be working around a live electrical line coming directly from a transformer."

Chalmers furrowed his brow, pursed his lips, and nodded. "Yes, of course, Sparky. Please come back on Monday morning, say around 9 a.m.? I will delay my departure for the office until later in the morning," Chalmers agreed.

"Monday morning it is," Sparky confirmed.

All it took for Seamus to know they were done for the day was a quick nod from Sparky. In less than fifteen minutes, they were packed and ready to go. Tools rattled in the duffel bags and the unused hardware rattled in crates for return to the hardware store for credit to Mr. Chalmers's account once the job was complete.

As they had done for other jobs in other cities, Sparky and Seamus kept some of the hardware from the blue-marked crate in reserve for their future jobs. Sparky didn't feel it was dishonest or unethical to keep a small portion of the excess hardware. Rather, it was always carried forward to the next job. "It all comes out in the wash," he would say.

"Seamus, I would rather you not go back to Allentown this weekend to see your wife," Sparky said as they worked their way back to the rooming house. "I can't afford the risk of you not making it back to Chambersburg in time for our Monday morning appointment at the Chalmers house."

"I wasn't planning on going back, Sparky. Bridgit and I have agreed that we should be apart for a while," Seamus explained. Sparky did not press him for further details.

On Monday, the electricians were at the Chalmers house a few minutes before nine a.m. They arrived well-fed, thanks to the rooming house's hearty breakfast, so there would be no delay while the household cook fed the two men a second breakfast. It was an important day and an important man like Chalmers did not like to be kept waiting.

By nine thirty, Sparky and Seamus had run the service line from the fuse box in the Chalmers cellar to the transformer across the street. It had been prearranged with the college for the transformer to be cut off long enough to make the Chalmers connection, which Sparky had estimated for no longer than fifteen minutes.

While Sparky was up on the ladder, Chalmers stood below, peppering Sparky with questions. It was slowing down the work and Sparky was becoming irritated. The distractions also had the potential to compromise Sparky's safety.

Seamus sensed Sparky's irritation and began explaining to Chalmers what was happening. Seamus figured that he could keep Chalmers occupied with a steady stream of babble, even if it wasn't entirely correct. Chalmers was, despite his wealth, a relatively uneducated man. Whenever he encountered someone who professed knowledge of something as complicated as electricity, he would defer to their opinions, correct or not.

At precisely nine-thirty, Sparky pulled the plunger on the cut-out switch on the hot side of the transformer and again for the switch on the supply side. The college went dark immediately. Working as quickly as he could, Sparky connected the hot and ground wires to the buss bar that would supply the Chalmers house with electricity.

Within fifteen minutes, the task was complete, and Sparky engaged the switches in reverse order. With both switches now live, power flowed through the wires, restoring electricity to the college and providing electricity to the Chalmers home for the first time. Sparky climbed down from the ladder and went inside to check that the three fuses had not blown from the sudden surge of power coming down the line. They were intact.

As he had done with all of his other wiring jobs, Sparky gave the homeowner and the senior household staff a tour and explanation of the capabilities of electricity. He was not, however, as graphic as he was when he explained the dangers to young Henry Frankel in Harrisburg.

Sparky demonstrated each switch and outlet for Mr. Chalmers and his wife, finishing around eleven a.m. when Chalmers had to leave for a meeting in his office. Afterwards, Sparky taught the servants how to change the bulbs in the overhead fixtures. Through all of his teaching, Sparky emphasized safety and shock prevention, making sure there were no frayed cords or loose cover plates.

The Chalmers house was only the beginning of their work in Chambersburg. Word traveled quickly in the small town and people were lining up to contract with Sparky to bring electricity to their homes. Only the poorest of the poor lacked the financial means to pay for Sparky's services, but he somehow managed to find a way to cover the costs out of the profits from the upper crust of Chambersburg society. He could have just as easily asked for handouts from people like Chalmers, but that would take all the fun out of Sparky's conscious efforts to redistribute the means across a broader swatch of society.

Chapter Nine: Meanwhile, in Harrisburg...
Late Spring, 1907

The older Henrietta Frankel got, the more demanding she became. She was no longer under the tutelage of a governess and well into the age where she should have been in finishing school. Adelaide Frankel was herself an alumna of Miss Porter's School in Farmington, Connecticut, and Henrietta was granted a legacy acceptance.

After one academic year at Miss Porter's School, young Henrietta was invited not to return. She had, during her short residency, discovered pleasures that involved illicit consumption of alcohol, use of tobacco, and providing certain favors to males of similar standing in society. It was enough that the Head of School wrote a sternly worded letter to her parents which unequivocally stated that Henrietta would not be allowed to return.

Upon reading the letter, Adelaide was distraught and inconsolable. Her daughter had embarrassed the family. Adelaide would not be able to look the other society ladies in the eye without seeing their haughty condemnation of her as a failed mother. Their own daughters, after all, always graduated from finishing schools with high marks and the most refined social graces, ready to become wives to the next generation of business moguls.

Adelaide knew that, without a finishing school diploma, Henrietta would be overlooked by the up-and-coming captains of industry. "If Henrietta were to marry at all," Adelaide said to Isaiah one evening, "it likely would be to a skilled tradesman, where the only thing expected of her would be to keep a clean house, have a hot meal waiting on the table each evening, and to produce children one after the other." Little did she know that her remarks were already as close to the truth as they could get.

Seamus Conaty had returned to Harrisburg on several occasions since he and Sparky had completed their work. One of his stops in Harrisburg was always the Frankel summer home. There, he talked his way into going through the house to inspect the wiring and make sure that everything was safe. It was during these visits that he had somehow gotten the attention of young Henrietta, who was not quite seventeen years old.

Seamus was already in his twenties and married to Bridgit. Because they were raised as Catholics and their marriage had been consummated, both divorce and annulment were out of the question. Bridgit was the most adamant about keeping her "until death us do part" vow, and in one of their heated disagreements with Seamus, he screamed, "Well, I wish you would hurry up and get there!" She suddenly realized that her attachment to Seamus was no longer anything other than a legal entanglement.

Somehow, Henrietta pried the facts out of Seamus and quickly figured out that he was married in name only. She also recognized that he could be easily seduced despite her age. Her off-campus experiences at Miss Porter's School had provided her with knowledge of certain intimate details that would have men wrapped around her finger.

At first, Seamus felt no guilt over his involvement with the young Miss Frankel. He couldn't even bring himself to call her by her first name without the "Miss" in front of it. It was always "Miss Frankel" or "Miss Henrietta," never just plain "Henrietta." Their trysts, though infrequent, became more and more physical, always stopping short of penetration. No matter how much Henrietta pleaded and offered her body, Seamus always declined.

"Miss Henrietta," he sighed, "it wouldn't be right for us to... you know..."

"No, I don't 'know,' Seamus. What are you talking about?" she teased.

"I'm still a married man and it just wouldn't be right," he tried to explain.

Henrietta had heard enough of his resistance and decided that she would have to resort to extreme measures. "Seamus Conaty, if you don't finish what we've started, I will tell my father that you already had taken my honor, true or not. Let's just see how long you last in Harrisburg after that!" she scolded.

The silence between the two of them was tense. Seamus knew he had to say or do something to keep this strumpet in line long enough to extricate himself from a scandalous predicament. He fidgeted for several minutes before offering an answer.

"Miss Henrietta," he said meekly, "I will be back in Harrisburg in two weeks' time. If you will wait for me, we can... uhh..."

"Yes, Seamus. I know what you are saying," she interrupted. "Of course, I can wait. But... I warn you... if you don't come through this time, I *will* tell my father."

Henrietta stormed to her private bathroom and slammed the door, leaving Seamus alone in her bedroom where he was allegedly working on the light switch. She was still nothing more than a petulant teenager, albeit a worldly one, and Seamus had come to expect a tantrum whenever he sidestepped *the issue* that was most important to her.

Seamus had observed that Henrietta, because of her expulsion from Miss Porter's School, was no longer afforded any attention from the household servants. Adelaide was punishing her, ostensibly training her daughter for survival on her own outside the umbrella of a well-to-do family. It was the source of considerable tension in the house, and the fact that Adelaide knew of Henrietta's attempted dalliances with Seamus added to the tension.

Before her wasted year at finishing school, Henrietta would rely on a servant to do every menial and manual task for her, including turning on a light switch. Not anymore. She had to do things for herself – meaning that the servants were no longer at her beck and call. Seamus had taken in this little tidbit of information as he finished his work on the switch.

Seamus replaced the cover plate on the light switch and packed up his tools. "Goodbye, Miss Henrietta," he called through the bathroom door as he turned to leave. It would be two weeks before he was back in Harrisburg and drawn to the wiles of Miss Henrietta Frankel.

Before boarding the train, Seamus stopped at a public telephone booth in the grand hall of the train station. From there, he placed a call to the Butler mansion in Allentown. Mrs. MacDonald answered and, after Seamus had identified himself as Bridgit's husband, sent one of the other servants to fetch Bridgit from her duties.

"Hello, my love," Seamus began. "I won't be making it to Allentown for a few more weeks. We are just too busy for me to be away for any longer than to attend Mass on Sunday."

"I understand, Seamus," Bridgit replied. She was becoming accustomed to his continued excuses for being away. She suspected he was spending time in the arms of another woman but did not press the issue. She, too, had been tempted on more than one occasion.

Their conversation continued for another five minutes with long pauses between their exchanges. They had very little to talk about other than their work and the distance between them was growing beyond the physical separation their jobs required.

"I wish I were a Protestant right now," Bridgit mused to herself. "They don't condemn divorce the way the Pope and the Catholic Church do." It was a surprise even to herself that she was considering an end to their marriage.

The evening train to Chambersburg arrived just after ten p.m. Seamus got off the train and headed for the boarding house a few blocks away. When he reached the shared room, he found Sparky sitting on the side of his bed reading the Bible, a book that the landlady made sure was in every room.

When Seamus entered, Sparky noticed a hint of that unique fragrance again. It was the same one he had detected a few weeks earlier when Seamus had ostensibly gone back to Allentown to visit Bridgit. The scent was still so familiar; he just couldn't identify where he had encountered it before. Again, he put the thought of Seamus being in a compromising relationship out of his mind and got ready for bed.

Seamus walked down the hall to the shared bathroom and washed himself to prepare for bed. He had been traveling all evening and the flop house where he had been staying in Harrisburg was lacking in sanitary facilities. The best it could offer was a very inefficient flush toilet and a sink with no hot water. He missed the "superior" accommodations that Sparky always managed to provide for their extended stays.

In Harrisburg, the disgraced Henrietta Frankel, too, was readying herself for bed. She started to call for one of the servants to help her undress but stopped herself in mid-utterance. She was, by her mother's edict, no longer receiving assistance from any of the servants and it was an ingrained habit of many years for her to call for help. She would have to learn how to do things on her own.

Henrietta drew herself a hot bath, undressed, and spent the next 30 minutes lounging in the hot water. Standing up as the water drained from the tub, she realized that she had forgotten to put a towel or her dressing gown within arm's reach of the tub. Up to this point, a servant would have been there to hand Henrietta a towel and even to help her dry off.

As the last of the bathwater circled the drain in a maelstrom, Henrietta got out of the tub and took the few steps across the bathroom to where a stack of luxuriously thick towels was arranged. She took one from the stack and dried herself, then put on her dressing gown and cinched it at the waist. In one smooth motion, she opened the bathroom door into her bedroom and almost unconsciously reached for the light switch – the one that Seamus had just installed – to turn off the bathroom light. The bathroom instantly went dark, and Henrietta made her way to the feather bed piled high with pillows and blankets which she now had to fluff and straighten for herself.

Reaching under her pillow, she pulled out a copy of *"My Secret Life,"* which she had purloined from her father's study. The stories in the book were titillating and described in graphic detail what went on in the houses of prostitution in Victorian London. The book was written from a male perspective, but Henrietta could fill in the blanks on the female point of view from her vivid imagination.

Her last waking moments focused on Seamus and their times together. It was Seamus she wanted. His muscled working-man's body... his mop of auburn hair... his complete lack of social grace, unlike the other men she was expected to consort with. It was Seamus she couldn't totally have – yet. She was obsessed with Seamus, and she would have him, or to daddy she would go.

As her sleep deepened, Henrietta's dreams went to his promise of returning in a fortnight. The dreams provided vivid images of their impending tryst. Though sound asleep, she moaned with desire and the thought of what would transpire between the two of them when he finally returned. In her dream, she could feel him next to her and on top of her, the sounds of their passion absorbed and muffled by the luxurious feather bed.

Chapter Ten: The Whole Damn Town
Summer, 1907

Chambersburg became the most lucrative of any of the towns that Sparky and Seamus had visited since their partnership began. The authorities engaged Sparky's services to electrify as many of the upper-class residential neighborhoods as possible, and Sparky continued his *pro bono* work to electrify sections of working-class neighborhoods. They were also asked to bring electricity to the more prominent businesses in town and to work with the shopkeepers to bring them into the electric age.

The pace of the work was so frenetic that Sparky took on a second apprentice, Michael Cooper. Mikey, as his parents called him, had grown up on one of the local farms and was not particularly drawn to the farming life. He did what his father told him to do, nothing more. Mikey had completed the Eighth Grade in public school, which was customary for farming families as "high school" was still reserved for families of means.

Mikey was both a quick learner and dedicated worker. Barely sixteen years old, he was not afraid to climb ladders, or to crawl into tight spaces. Working around live electrical lines didn't make him nervous at all. Sparky saw potential in the young man and hoped that someday Mikey could become a journeyman electrician. Not that Sparky had any misgivings about Seamus's abilities, either, but Seamus did like his drink and his women – both of which could easily distract him from the job at hand.

"Mikey… Seamus… we have another job to do," Sparky said one Monday morning after the trio met outside the boarding house. "It is a larger home on the east side of town. Electricity has already been run along the Gettysburg Road and we will have to run a line north from there to the new mansion. It was just finished a couple of years ago, and the owner wants electricity… he knows Mr. Chalmers quite well and is willing to pay us handsomely for our troubles."

"What about all of the working families' homes?" Seamus asked.

"We will set them aside for now, finishing the ones we have already started, then go out to the new job. It shouldn't take us any longer than it did to wire Mr. Chalmers's home," Sparky explained.

Seamus dissented with this approach. "Here we are again bowing to the whims of rich people while sacrificing the working man." His voice oozed sarcasm.

"Seamus Conaty, I remind you that you are in my employ and that it is up to me to determine in what order we do our work, Besides, the rich people pay us, handsomely I might add, and we do the factory workers' homes for next to nothing." Sparky reprimanded.

"Yes, sir," Seamus responded with an air of contempt in his voice.

As they left the boarding house, the newsboy on the corner was hawking the morning papers.

"Read all about it!" he shouted, "Daughter of Harrisburg Magnate Dead from Electrocution!" The newsboy drew out each syllable, "ee-lec-tro-cuu-shunnn," for emphasis. News of happenings in Harrisburg, the state capital, was of interest across the state and Chambersburg was no exception.

Seamus blanched when he heard the headline. Henrietta's threats to tell her father about them were no longer of concern. She was apparently dead, and dead women certainly couldn't tell their fathers any lies. Still, it was another death that could be laid at Seamus's feet.

"Son, let me have one of those papers," Sparky said.

"Of course, sir. That will be five cents," the newsboy responded.

"Here, keep the change!" said Sparky, tossing the boy a dime.

Finding a bench in the corner park, Sparky sat down to read the newspaper article aloud to Seamus and Mikey:

*"**Harrisburg:** Miss Henrietta Frankel, daughter of rail and steel tycoon Isaiah Frankel, was found dead in her bedroom yesterday morning, the victim of an apparently accidental electrocution. Miss Frankel was just barely seventeen years of age. The Dauphin County Coroner has taken the body into care and will ascertain the cause of death. The incident happened at the Frankel family's summer home on a hill overlooking the city.*

Miss Frankel is survived by her parents, Isaiah and Adelaide (nee Kleinschmitt) Frankel, and her brothers, Henry and William. The family is in mourning and asks that well-wishers respect their privacy until funeral arrangements are complete."

Seamus's mind raced. With Henrietta gone, could he move on with his life and go back to Bridgit without feeling guilty? Would someone connect him to Henrietta's demise? Did he do something wrong when he installed the electrical hardware? He put those thoughts out of his mind before speaking.

"Sparky, didn't we wire the Frankel summer home last fall?" Seamus asked; he already knew the answer.

"Yes, we did. I suppose someone there didn't heed my instructions," Sparky replied. "I spent quite a while explaining the dangers of electricity to Master Henry Frankel. I was vividly descriptive in my explanation, telling him about the electric chair designed by Dr. Southwick. He was so scared that he wet himself."

"Do you think we should down tools and go to Harrisburg to investigate?" Seamus asked.

Sparky nervously rubbed the back of his neck as he thought about the answer. "No. It would not be a good idea for us to go back there. We could get blamed, even if there was nothing wrong," Sparky replied. "Once that rumor starts, we would no longer be welcome in Harrisburg. Besides, we have work to be done here in Chambersburg."

After meeting with the mansion's owner, Mr. Henry Langston, Sparky came up with a plan. They would use a process similar to what they had done for the Chalmers house, fitting out each room with switches, outlets, and light fixtures, before bringing full electrical service to the new fuse box in the well-appointed cellar. Sparky estimated that it would take them the better part of two weeks to place the fixtures.

Mikey was so new to electricity that he barely understood the difference between a switch and an outlet. His family farmhouse still was lit by candle or oil lamps; it was west of town and electrical service had not yet reached that section. Providing electrical service that far west would prove problematic in time, as there was a band of Amish farms between town and the Cooper homestead. The Amish would oppose giving any easement to modern conveniences.

It fell to Seamus, now the senior apprentice, to teach Mikey the names of all the pieces of hardware they would use for this very large house. "This is a switch," he explained. "It interrupts a circuit and turns off power down the line." Mikey nodded in understanding as Seamus continued his lecture for the next thirty minutes. The lecture over, Seamus sent Mikey to fetch the equipment they would need from their pushcart.

Back and forth Mikey ran with armloads of electrical parts. He moved quickly through the house, placing two outlets, a switch, and a light fixture from the red crate in each room that was to receive electricity. Mr. Langston had also made provisions for the servants' quarters to be included in the electrification but not to the extent that the main house was being fitted. The servants lived in dormitory-style accommodations at the rear of the house and each of the rooms was to be fitted with a single overhead light and a single outlet, which Seamus explained, "come from the blue crate." Langston did not want to provide the servants with anything more than was necessary.

*　　*　　*　　*　　*

In Allentown, Doctor Mittford was sitting down to read the morning papers at the gentlemen's club. It was part of his daily ritual to take his coffee in one of the overstuffed leather chairs nearest a window that overlooked the kitchen herb garden. The club regulars knew not to occupy that seat when Doctor Mittford was in town.

Even seated, Doctor Robert Mittford was an imposing and solemn figure. His hair was always impeccably coiffed. He rarely ventured out in public without an immaculate shave – which he did himself using a straight razor. His collars were always starched and his neckwear precisely tied and positioned. Mittford believed that such attention to detail was important for a man of medicine.

Doctor Mittford also made sure that his body was in prime condition. He relished any opportunity to engage in manual labor and his physique showed its results. Well-muscled and firm, more than one of Allentown's eligible young ladies found themselves atwitter after seeing him chopping firewood. Mittford had been presented with plenty of opportunities for female companionship, but remained single as he felt that a wife and family would distract him from his first love, medicine.

The club's subscriptions included the Harrisburg paper, as most of the club's members had a vested interest in the happenings at the state capitol. Lifting the morning's "Harrisburg Courier" from the stack, the headline immediately caught his eye:

Henrietta Frankel Electrocuted

The item above the fold on the front page read almost identically to the one that Sparky had read to his two apprentices in Chambersburg earlier that morning. Mittford was puzzled. It was the second electrocution suffered by a high-born family with whom he had a connection.

Mittford knew a few details about the Frankel family, having attended university with Isaiah Frankel in the early 1890s. After commencement, their lives diverged and Mittford headed immediately for medical school in New York. Their paths crossed in Harrisburg from time to time, and Isaiah Frankel was always proud to share news of his family.

"Losing his only daughter must be devastating," Mittford thought to himself. He also remembered the incident at the Butler mansion. "Is this a pattern?" he said aloud as he furrowed his brow.

Mittford remembered being accosted a second time by Sean Mulcahy when he pressed the County Coroner for more information on Edgar Allan Butler's death in spite of a previous warning. Mulcahy's words still haunted Mittford: "For the last time, back away from the County Coroner and don't ask anymore questions. A doctor needs his hands, and it would be a shame if anything happened to them." Doctor Mittford knew Mulcahy meant business; it was not an empty threat.

Once again, Doctor Mittford's mind was racing. Challenging the County Coroner was out of the question, with Sean Mulcahy's not-so-veiled threats standing in the way. Making a statement to the Sherriff was also off the table. He, too, was a Butler man, bought off after the last election. Doc Mittford was in a quandary.

Rather than bucking against Waldo Emerson Butler's control of Allentown, Mittford decided to put his skills as a researcher to good use. There had to be answers to the question of what caused the two published electrocutions in Allentown and Harrisburg. He also suspected there were others, from among the less privileged classes, that did not always make it into the papers.

Mittford's patient list was limited to the wealthiest families of Allentown, nearly all of whom went away to summer homes as soon as their children returned home from boarding schools. Only the husbands, the so-called "captains of industry," remained behind. This provided an ideal opportunity for Mittford to take a vacation as well – only it would not be a vacation in the relaxation context.

He would be working, but it would not be to treat the venereal diseases of the rich men who chose to stray while their wives were away for the summer. Instead, he would be in the Harrisburg library poring over stacks and stacks of newspapers from as far away as Baltimore, trying to determine if there was a pattern to the electrocutions.

Mittford read that there were two electrocutions in the Lawyers Hill and Relay areas south of Baltimore. Both were suffered by the nearly adult children of "old money" Maryland families during the summer of 1905. Another detail was staring him in the face: the area was serviced by a spur of the Pennsylvania Railroad, with a passenger stop specifically constructed to serve the summer homes of the wealthy.

As his mind raced through the possibilities, the railroad connection crystallized as more than a coincidence. Mittford also noted that the electrocutions, reported by the County Medical Examiners to be accidental, all happened within two or three weeks of the residence receiving electrical service.

"That's odd," Mittford said to himself, "near a rail line… new electrical service… happening two or three weeks after the job was done, and the Lawyers Hill incidents happened a while before Allentown and Harrisburg. This is more than a coincidence!"

*   *   *   *   *

The job at the Langston mansion was completed ahead of schedule and under budget, but Sparky did not adjust his quoted price of two thousand dollars. It was rare that the wealthy negotiated for a lower price and generally accepted what Sparky quoted, Henry Langston was no different. The rich businessmen, as Sparky put it, "were too busy to be bothered" with investigating the fine points of electrical service or apprentice wages. Besides, most of them believed in the adage that "if you have to ask what it costs, you can't afford it."

Through his salesmanship, Sparky was becoming wealthy himself, even after donating at least ten percent of his profits to philanthropic causes. He paid Seamus nearly double what he would have made in a union job. Mikey, too, was making enough to send money home to his parents. It was money they sorely needed to keep the farm afloat.

Sparky knew it was time for them to take finer accommodations than the boarding house near the Old Jail. He now had the wherewithal to rent a suite of rooms in a mid-level hotel on the outskirts of town. It was finely appointed with fresh wallpaper, crisp linens, and pastel colors. "We're moving up in the world," Sparky would tell his apprentices when their jaws dropped at the opulence of their new, albeit temporary, home. They had known nothing better than rooming houses since they came into Sparky's employ.

Leaving the apprentices to unpack in their smaller, but still adequate, rooms, Sparky returned to the front desk. The hotelier, with a well-groomed and graying moustache and beard that Sparky found amusing, proposed a barter arrangement for Sparky's accommodations. Instead of a cash payment for two months' room and board for the three men, the hotelier proposed that Sparky wire the hotel for electricity free of charge.

Without hesitation, Sparky seized the opportunity. Separate rooms meant no more listening to Seamus snore at night nor smelling the remnants of his dalliances with the ladies. No more eating second-rate boiled beef and potatoes in a local tavern. No more drinking watered down beer. It wouldn't be long before he was invited to hobnob with the moneyed gentry of Chambersburg.

After Sparky and his team were ensconced in the hotel, they returned to the tasks of electrifying it and as much of Chambersburg as they could before the early stages of winter set in. It would, Sparky had calculated, coincide with the expiration of their two months' room and board. Then it would be time for them to move on.

Over breakfast the next morning, Sparky explained what was happening next and how they would be leaving Chambersburg in no more than two months. Seamus was always concerned that their travels would put him at odds with the law in either Baltimore or Harrisburg. Mikey, on the other hand. had never really been away from his family, so he began to worry about being far from his parents.

"Where should we go next, gentlemen?" Sparky asked, his voice full of energy.

"What if they need me? What if I get hurt?" This was just the start of Mikey's long litany of anxious concerns about leaving town. Sparky hoped that the anxiety would calm down as soon as they were on the road.

"Hagerstown is nearby, but they are already mostly electrified," Seamus observed. Hagerstown was close to a power plant and towns with such plants generally were fully electrified in short order once the plant started producing electricity. "What about Frederick?" he asked.

"Frederick… hmm…" Sparky mused. "We might as well be heading to Baltimore."

The mere mention of Baltimore made Seamus uneasy. He really did not want to ever go back to that town, as it was a reminder of a violent past. It had been nearly five years since he beat the foreman to death, making it unlikely that there was an open investigation, and even less likely that anyone there would remember him. Back then, he was just another Irishman passing through. "Micks are a dime a dozen but worth a lot less," the locals would say. Still, Seamus did not want to take the chance of ending up in prison for murder.

"What about Pittsburgh?" Mikey asked. "Weren't you heading there before you got stuck in Chambersburg?"

"Wherever we go, I need to let Bridgit know where we are headed," Seamus said, suddenly having a conscience. After the Henrietta Frankel incident, he was trying his best to stay on the straight and narrow. He just hoped that he would be able to patch things up with his wife. They had drifted so far apart in the past couple of years.

The three men were enjoying their second cup of coffee when a messenger walked into the dining room. "Message for Mister Archibald Thompson," he repeated three times, each time louder and more drawn out than the time before. Sparky got up and identified himself and the messenger handed him a sealed envelope. Sparky opened it and read the message silently.

"Mr. Thompson, the delivery wagon that you ordered has just been delivered to the train station. Please make your way there at your earliest opportunity." The note was signed by John French, the co-owner of the St. Louis Motor Carriage Company, operating out of Peoria, Illinois.

Returning to the table, barely able to contain his excitement, Sparky gushed, "Gentlemen, I have a surprise for you. If you will please follow me to the train station…"

A few minutes later, Sparky, Seamus, and Mikey were at the Chambersburg rail station. Sitting next to the platform was a gleaming new delivery truck. Mikey and Seamus could not believe their eyes. It meant that they would no longer be the beasts of burden pulling their equipment wagon all over town. Instead, they would fit out the delivery truck as a mobile workshop – with all the parts and wiring that they needed right there, organized to perfection.

"Seamus, Mikey…" Sparky said, his voice cracking with emotion. "It is because of your hard work that I have been able to purchase this fine vehicle. It will carry all three of us and our equipment from job to job and town to town."

Seamus and Mikey walked around the delivery truck in awe, caressing every inch of it as if it were a beautiful woman. Its black fenders gleamed. The engine was still pristine and devoid of the oil seepage that plagued most early internal combustion engines. The inside of the cargo box was still immaculate and spartan.

Seamus knew they would have to do some carpentry work to make it into a usable work wagon. Mikey, on the other hand, focused on the 4-cylinder engine and drive train. He had only read about gasoline engines and was fascinated that he could now examine one up close. "It is a work of art," Mikey gasped.

The sales literature had been left on the driver's seat. It claimed that the truck was capable of speeds up to 20 miles per hour and that its suspension would provide a safe ride for cargo over bumpy country roads. Neither of those statements would prove true a few hours later.

Sparky broke the silence after a few minutes: "Seamus, Mikey, we are going to Baltimore. I hear they are building a massive new power plant that will provide electricity to the entire city. Somebody has to do all of that wiring, and it might as well be us."

"Sparky, should we at least fit the inside of the cargo area with shelves and crates to keep our tools and supplies neat?" Seamus asked.

"Of course," Sparky replied. "As long as there is logic to the arrangements, I trust you and Mikey to get it done before we leave for Baltimore in the morning."

Seamus left the details of the carpentry up to Mikey. "Measure twice and cut once, my granddaddy would say," Mikey asserted as they took stock of the cargo box. It would, Mikey thought, be a relatively easy job.

The two apprentices spent the remainder of the afternoon building racks and shelves inside the cargo box. Mikey, however, did not consider that everything in the cargo box could shift as they maneuvered along the bumpy roads. In his ignorance, he neglected to build shelves that would keep equipment crates from sliding around or off the shelves into the center aisle.

Chapter Eleven: Baltimore... Again
Fall, 1907

The three men left Chambersburg at the end of the two-month hotel stay. It didn't take them long to load up the new delivery truck with their equipment and personal belongings. It was Sparky's truck, so he naturally was in the driver's seat. Seamus was seated to his right.

Mikey, as the junior member of the team, was relegated to the cargo box; he sat on his own duffel bag to cushion his backside from the rigors of the badly rutted roads. More than once, boxes of equipment crashed down around him, and he was quite fortunate not to be injured by the falling items. Mikey suddenly realized he had not accounted for such movement when he designed the shelves. Whenever the truck stopped, Mikey made sure that the same equipment would not fall again and noted what he would need to do to prevent the calamity from recurring in the future.

Unknown to Mikey, Seamus had very carefully sorted all of the electrical parts like outlets and switches into two groups: those for the homes of working men and those for the homes of the wealthy. The hardware meant for the working families' homes was in a crate marked with a blue stripe and the equipment for the wealthy was in a red-marked crate. When the equipment toppled off the shelves in the back of the truck, they were hopelessly intermingled. Seamus had not marked the equipment individually, thinking that separating them by storage bins in the truck would be sufficient. He did not anticipate the effects the constant jostling would have on their cargo, nor did he anticipate Mikey's ineptitude and haste to clean up the spilled gear.

Sitting in the driver's seat and totally unaware of the commotion in the cargo area behind him, Sparky noticed how few automobiles and trucks there were on the roads between towns. He had gotten accustomed to Chambersburg, where the town seemed at times to be overrun with delivery trucks and the automobile had begun to supplant horse-and-buggy travel. Chambersburg's roads within the city limits were mostly paved or at least packed gravel, a standard that rural roads were not even close to reaching.

Though advertised as capable of a higher speed, the fully loaded delivery truck could only manage a top speed of twelve miles per hour on level ground and labored to climb even the slightest hill. It would take them nearly all day to get to their overnight stopover in Westminster, Maryland – assuming, of course, that the truck did not break down nor have some other disabling mechanical malfunction. Sparky knew electricity, but he was far from expert on internal combustion engines or the mechanical components of the truck's chassis.

They had made it as far east as Gettysburg on what would in just a few more years be known as the Lincoln Highway when the first mechanical issue cropped up, a flat tire. Mikey, with his jack-of-all-trades farming background, instinctively knew how to jack up the truck, remove the wheel, pry the tire and tube from the wheel, patch the hole, and put things back together. Working as quickly as he could, it still took Mikey over an hour to get them back on the road again.

From Gettysburg, they continued southeast on the Littlestown Road, passing through verdant farmland and horse pastures, uneventfully reaching Littlestown not quite four hours later. It was there that the trio decided to stop at a roadhouse for a meal. Sparky could afford to take his group to a fine restaurant, but because they were only transients and would not have access to bathing facilities or fresh clothing, the roadhouse was the only realistic option.

Roadhouses were come-as-you-are affairs, catering to working men and travelers. Women were rarities in such establishments. The food was always filling, but not very imaginative. Meals consisted of a meat (usually a lesser quality cut of beef) and a selection of two or three root vegetables. Sometimes, it was a stockpot stew. Today, the Littlestown roadhouse was serving hearty beef stew, which the proprietor brought to the table in steaming bowls.

Sparky already knew they would not make Westminster before dark. The hour's delay for the flat tire meant that they would have to take whatever accommodation might be available. Fortunately, Westminster was home to seven hotels, and it was unlikely that they all would be full during the week. Sparky already knew from his conversations with the Chambersburg elite that the Winchester House was beyond his means and social standing. They would more likely take their overnight accommodation at the Anchor Inn, a working men's hotel that catered to transients.

Sparky, Seamus, and Mikey arrived at the Anchor just as the lamplighter was making his rounds to all the gaslights in the center of town. Westminster, Sparky observed, had still not fully accepted electricity as a modern convenience. "If it wasn't for our plan to go to Baltimore," he told his two apprentices, "we could stay here and make it another Chambersburg." A sly smile spread across his face.

Seamus was in favor of any opportunity that kept him away from Baltimore and his vivid memories of that alley near the Canton Company. He was afraid that someone might remember him and accuse him of the foreman's murder. Seamus did not know that the only witness, whose own story wasn't exactly watertight, was already dead.

Settling in for the night, Sparky took his own room and billeted Seamus and Mikey together. They were only staying for one night and it did not make economic sense to pay for three rooms when two would do. The two apprentices did not mind sharing accommodation, but Seamus now insisted that such an arrangement was only palatable as long as there were two single beds or a bed and a sofa in the room. Seamus had sensed from the start that there was something different about Mikey, and sharing a bed was just not going to happen.

By now, Mikey had been with Sparky's team for several months. He didn't seem at all interested in the tales of

Seamus's adulterous dalliances with the young ladies they had encountered in the homes of the wealthy. Mikey also demurred reciprocating the advances of a couple of attentive barmaids in the various Chambersburg establishments they frequented. Seamus thought Mikey's behavior was somewhat odd, but Sparky realized that Mikey had been kept on the farm his entire life and the only contact he had had with other people was with his immediate family and the polite encounters at church on Sundays. Everyone was always on their best behavior at church.

They arose the following morning, anxious to get back on the road to Baltimore, which was still more than forty miles distant. As they sat around the breakfast table, Seamus spoke of the opportunities that awaited them. Seamus and Mikey waited with bated breath.

"Gentlemen, the whole city of Baltimore awaits," Sparky said grandiloquently. "I believe we can be as successful there as we were in Chambersburg. Baltimore is much larger, but with many outlying areas where the wealthy reside, and electricity has not advanced beyond the downtown area," Sparky explained.

Seamus leaned in over the table, speaking *sotto voce*. "Sparky, it worries me to be going back to Baltimore," Seamus replied. He had no intention of discussing his past situation there as long as anyone else, especially the hotel staff, was within earshot. "Sparky," Seamus said, dropping his voice to a whisper, "if you will allow me the courtesy of explaining to you in private, it will be much appreciated."

A deadpan Sparky merely nodded and understood that Seamus was finally opening up about his past, something that Sparky had wanted for a long time. Seamus was an able apprentice and seemed to have had some skills from a previous situation that exported into domestic and industrial electrical work. Sparky really wanted to know more about the quiet, calculating Irishman – beyond the fact that he was married to Bridgit and had been flirtatiously involved with the now-deceased Henrietta Frankel.

As they finished their meal, Sparky went to the front desk to settle their account. He returned a few minutes later and motioned to his apprentices that it was time for them to be back on the road. "It will take us until mid-afternoon to reach Baltimore. I want us to have some sort of accommodation before nightfall," Sparky said. His tone made it clear that he was in charge.

The seating arrangement was as it was the previous day: Sparky at the wheel, Seamus in the passenger's seat, and Mikey in the cargo box behind them. Sparky was certain that it would be so noisy in the cargo box that Mikey would be unable to hear any conversation taking place in the front compartment.

"Seamus, I think it is time for you to tell me why you view Baltimore with such apprehension," Sparky said in an effort to open a more frank conversation.

Seamus looked out the window as he thought for a moment. He wanted to choose his next words carefully. "I killed a man in Baltimore," he said with no emotion or expression in his voice. He waited for Sparky to digest that tidbit of information and respond before giving any more details. As if on cue, a large rut in the road suddenly bounced the truck on its suspension as if to emphasize Seamus's statement.

"Killed a man? How? Why?" Sparky's voice trembled as he queried his apprentice for more details.

"It was not long after we got off the ship coming from Ireland," Seamus began. "I had found work with a company in Baltimore, but the foreman – though his surname was Murphy – had a hatred of anything Irish. I had been employed there for just a few weeks and he pushed me over the edge with his never-ending insults…"

Sparky digested what he had just been told. His apprentice had not once shown a mean or homicidal tendency, something that Sparky found curious and a little unsettling. *"Perhaps Seamus is just good at hiding his emotions and controlling his temper,"* Sparky thought to himself.

When the road did not require Sparky's undivided mental and physical attention, Seamus provided more details about his origins. He recounted the stint at the Harland-Wolff shipyard and his difficulties there but elaborated more on the experiences he gained with electrical work.

"I have often wondered if you had worked with an electrician before," Sparky commented as they passed through Reisterstown. "You picked things up so quickly, and I assumed at first that it was natural talent. Now you've confirmed my suspicion."

By the time they reached the Baltimore city limits, Seamus had told his entire story, including his current estrangement from Bridgit. "Sparky, you have to promise me that you will keep what I have told you in confidence," Seamus pleaded. "The last thing I want is for Mikey to find out anything about my past. He seems so naïve and unaware of worldly things. I sometimes wonder if he has no interest in the fairer sex…"

"Everything you have told me will stay with me," Sparky assured his apprentice. "I don't want to lose your talents. I have come to depend on you as much as I do my own right hand."

Sparky had some previous familiarity with Baltimore and headed to the southeast side of town, Near the Camden rail station, at 406 Conway Street, was a saloon and rooming house owned by George Ruth. It was fortunate that Ruth was between tenants, as he usually only rented rooms to newly-arrived German immigrants. It had been several weeks since the last ship had arrived from Bremen.

Sparky was put in the room once occupied by Ruth's son, George, Junior, who had been legally committed to St. Mary's Industrial School for Boys about five years earlier.

Seamus and Mikey were assigned an attic room that, fortunate for Seamus, was fitted out with two twin beds.

Baltimore's "Pigtown" was known for its rooming houses, immigrant population, butcher shops, and railroad workers. It was never quiet and always boisterous. Barroom brawls were common, as was petty theft. Sparky hoped they would not have to stay there for very long, despite very little of Pigtown having been fitted for electric service, Ruth's saloon included.

Sparky knew the money was going to come from the upscale neighborhoods in and outside the city. He also recognized that there were Negro neighborhoods clamoring for attention and modern conveniences. Sparky had no prejudices when it came to revenue sources.

"Colored money is just as good as white money," he told Seamus and Mikey when they took a job for the Marshall family on Division Street. Mrs. Marshall, a schoolteacher, was heavily pregnant; her husband, a railroad porter, wanted the house to have electricity before the baby was born. Their first child was born three years earlier by candlelight and the Marshalls did not want that same situation for their next child.

Sparky focused his work on the rowhouses of Baltimore, with the occasional sojourn into the more affluent white neighborhoods and towns surrounding the city. The first of these properties was a Victorian manor house in Arbutus. The owner, a Mr. Crampton, was just like all of the other wealthy people that Sparky had done work for in the past.

"Mr. Crampton," Sparky said, scratching his chin for emphasis as he jotted notes with his pencil, "all together, I estimate it will cost around a thousand dollars to wire your home with electricity. That's the basic price, including labor, that will give you one light fixture and one receptacle per room."

Sparky knew that these wealthy businessmen would not question the price nor ask for an itemized breakdown of the bill. They simply took at face value the estimates that tradesmen provided, and Crampton's dealing with Sparky was no different. Crampton simply pursed his lips and nodded his assent for Sparky to continue.

"We'll start work on Tuesday," Sparky said. "I need the next four days to gather the necessary equipment."

"Certainly," Crampton replied.

What Sparky had left unsaid was that he already had all of the equipment stockpiled in the back of his truck. He only needed to purchase the wire itself – which was the least expensive part of the job – before starting the project.

Returning to their rooming house in Baltimore, Sparky treated his apprentices to some of the Ruth's finest local beer. "Gentlemen," he said as he raised his glass, "to our continued success and to our wealthy customers!"

"Hear, Hear!" Seamus and Mikey responded.

"Mr. Ruth, a round for the house if I may?" Sparky ordered. The saloon was not fully occupied, as it was late on a Thursday afternoon and most of the factories and slaughterhouses had not yet sounded their end-of-day whistles. In the end, Sparky was only out of pocket for about six mugs of beer.

The end-of-day whistles always made Seamus tremble. They brought back nightmarish memories of his previous time in Baltimore and the abrupt encounter with the police officer with the scarred face. Seamus hoped that remaining in Baltimore would not end with him being put in jail for Michael Murphy's murder.

Chapter Twelve: All Lit Up
1907-1908

Baltimore's residents took pride in the appearance of their neighborhoods. Consisting mostly of pressed-brick rowhomes, the woman of each house kept their front steps spotless, making the Cockeysville marble gleam. It didn't matter what the neighborhood's ethnicity was; it was a matter of pride for the women to showcase their ability to keep house. "If my front stoop's not clean, hon, my house ain't clean, neither!' was commonly heard throughout the city. Even women that worked outside the home made sure that their marble stoops were just as clean as those of women who stayed home. Scrubbing the steps was almost a ritual for some of the women.

Just like Chambersburg, Harrisburg, and Allentown, Baltimore was becoming a goldmine for Sparky and his two apprentices. They worked six days a week, often more than twelve hours a day, bringing electricity to homes that could afford it – as well as some that couldn't. Sparky's business model always allowed some of the rates he charged the wealthy businessmen to offset his *pro bono publica* and reduced-rate work in the blue-collar neighborhoods.

After several weeks of working at a breakneck pace, Sparky decided that it would be a good idea to take on a general laborer who could work his way up to an apprenticeship. Every day, time was wasted taking either Seamus or Mikey away from snaking wires or connecting devices to unload equipment and tools from the truck.

"Mikey, Seamus..." Sparky began over dinner at the Ruth saloon one evening, "we need to take on another worker. A laborer who will work his way up to an apprenticeship. We are too busy to have the two of you interrupting your work for menial tasks like loading and unloading our truck at both ends of the day."

"That sounds good to me," Seamus responded.

"That means I won't be the new guy anymore?" Mikey said, grinning sheepishly from ear to ear.

"You are both correct," Sparky answered. "I do have to tell you that our new man will be from the colored neighborhood on Division Street. The people there are proud of their community, and I can think of no better way to recognize that pride than to take one of their own people into our employment."

Seamus spoke first. "Boss, you know this will get all kinds of attention from the fekin' rich white people we work for. They are not likely to let a colored man, no matter who he works for, into their homes even while he is moving our equipment so that we can work on their mansions." The tone in Seamus's voice was sharp and spiteful.

"I know exactly what you are saying, Seamus," Sparky responded, "and we will have to deal with that when the time comes... For now, I will be hiring Willie Washington... he lives next door to the Marshall family and has been out of work for a few months. His family certainly could use the money from a steady job."

"I know who you are talking about," said Seamus. "He's always polite and seems to be well-educated. As long as he turns out to be reliable..."

"I have to take him at his word, Seamus. He told me that he was fired from his last job because a white man accused him of stealing. I don't believe it for a minute, as I have left our truck wide open while we work and Willie has not gone anywhere near the equipment crates in the back, not even out of curiosity."

"It's settled, then..." Seamus agreed with a quick nod, and Mikey seconded with a nod of his own.

As they were finishing up the work on the Marshall home, Sparky offered Willie the job. It took Willie less than a minute to accept.

"Mr. Thompson," Willie began, "I've been out of work long enough that my family is eating on the good graces of others, especially Mr. and Mrs. Marshall. My wife, Charity, takes in washing and sewing for pin money. Our little ones are not yet in school, so she has them to deal with all day as well. I tries to help, but if I am there with them, I am not out looking for work."

"Willie, instead of paying you for the first two weeks you work for me, I am offering you the chance to have your home electrified at no charge while we evaluate your trustworthiness. Regardless of that outcome, your home will have electricity," Sparky said, extending his hand for a handshake. He did not even mention the possibility of an apprenticeship, as he did not want to falsely build hopes for Willie; after all, the man was untested and had been hired solely based on their initial evaluations of his character.

"Mr. Thompson, I am much obliged to you for your generous offer," Willie replied as he firmly shook Sparky's hand.

"Willie, you can call me 'Sparky'. Everyone else does… well… everyone except the rich people who insist on formalities."

"Yessir, Sparky/ I can do that," Willie said, his elation at finally being employed shining through. "It will be nice to be able to feed my family again."

It was quitting time on Friday. "You start on Monday. We will be here at 8 o'clock to start working on your home," Sparky said, smiling.

Willie ran up the steps to his rowhome. "Charity! I got a job! Sparky, the electric man working on the Marshall place… he's giving me a job and we are… getting electricity!" Willie's face shone with excitement as he danced a little jig around his somewhat skeptical wife.

"Willie, are you sure you want to work for a white man again? The last time… you were…" Charity began to respond, briefly dampening her husband's enthusiasm.

"This is different, Sweets. Sparky… Mr., Thompson actually shook my hand. No white man has ever done that before, least not as part of a gentleman's agreement," Willie responded, immediately silencing Charity's objection. "I start on Monday."

As Sparky promised, he, Seamus, and Mikey arrived promptly at 8 a.m. on Monday. It fell to Mikey to show Willie the ropes. "This box, the one with the blue marking, is the equipment we use for working men's homes. The one with the red mark is for the rich folk," Mikey explained. "This is a switch…" He held one up, then put it right back down again. "This is an outlet…" again, he showed Willie the device. "Over here, we have our wires and insulators."

Mikey spent the next half-hour explaining to Willie what they would need for each portion of the day's work to wire the Washington house. Willie was dispatched multiple times to the truck for gear, returning each time with total accuracy.

"Seamus," Mikey whispered after he had sent Willie to the truck for the fourth time, "he's catching on quickly!"

"I can see that," Seamus replied. "I'll tell Sparky that he made a good choice to hire Willie. Let's hope he keeps up the good work."

At the end of the first week, Willie's work and work ethic convinced Sparky to pay Willie half of the wages he would otherwise have been entitled to, had they not been electrifying the Washington's rowhome for free. "Good work deserves to be rewarded," Sparky told Willie as he handed over the pay envelope. Inside was a crisp ten dollar bill. "Don't say anything to Seamus and Mikey; though."

Sparky, Willie assessed, was a fair-minded white man worthy of admiration. The grandson of escaped slaves, Willie had seen the horrific patchwork of scars on his grandfather's back, scars that came from an overseer's whip on a plantation on Virginia's Northern Neck. His grandmother had died in childbirth when Willie's own father was born not long after the end of the Civil War. The family ended up in Baltimore ahead of the Great Migration that would come a few years later.

Willie had been brought up to distrust whites and to always be deferential and polite. Yet here he was, faced with a white boss who didn't care what color a man's skin was – if he was honest and worked hard. Willie had every intention of keeping Sparky's trust.

Just after dark that Friday, Willie went home to Charity and the children. He was smiling from ear to ear as he showed his wife the fruits of a week's labor. "All that just for helping wire my own house!" he exclaimed.

"Hush, now!" Charity said. "Don't be bragging about that money or your boss might just take it back…"

"Mister Thompson… Sparky… is a good man," Willie replied. "He doesn't have a hateful bone in his body, least not towards this family, anyway.

Over the next few weeks, Sparky and his team alternated between a "colored neighborhood" and the homes of rich white people. On more than one occasion, the lady of the house suggested that Willie could not be trusted in their homes. Sparky heard, more than once, "But he's colored… and they will steal us blind!" Just as often, Sparky would hear the rich people mutter "nigger lover" under their breath.

Sparky did his best to dispel the prejudicial notions held by white housewives in Baltimore, especially the well-to-do. He had to explain over and over again that his own standards were impeccable, and that Willie could be trusted in all circumstances. Most, however, could not get over their distrust of black men. Whenever and wherever Willie was working, a servant or family member was always watching. Watching and making sure that Willie did not steal anything or get anywhere near their teen-age daughters.

The first neighborhood where Sparky and his team encountered the overt white prejudices was Ruxton Heights, an emerging wealthy neighborhood north of the city. It was served by a branch line of the Baltimore and Susquehanna Railroad, making it easily accessible for the doctors of The Johns Hopkins Hospital or the lawyers and industrialists of Baltimore. As the summer homes went up, Sparky found it much easier to add electricity within the walls as the homes were being built, rather than adding wires and other electrical hardware after-the-fact.

"Willie, go out to the truck and get me five switches, ten outlets, and ten light fixtures," Sparky ordered as they started work on one Ruxton Heights summer home. "Be sure you get the ones from the crate with the red marking."

"Yes, Sparky!" Willie quickly replied.

"Sparky, what's so special about the stuff in the crate marked with red?" Seamus asked. Mikey heard the question and instantly became attentive to the emerging conversation. He, too, was curious about the distinction between the two crates, but for a completely different reason.

"Seamus, the hardware in that crate is sent to me directly from Mr. Edison's plant in New Jersey." Sparky chose not to explain the entirety of the process just yet. He gave Seamus (and Mikey, by his proximity) just enough information to answer the question. He didn't explain how John Garfield came about getting the hardware, nor that it was purloined from Edison. Sparky needed to keep that part of the arrangement secret for the time being.

Sparky was paying Garfield less than wholesale price for the electrical hardware, money that Garfield was pocketing. What Sparky didn't know was that Garfield was not stealing the hardware from the assembly line; rather, that he was sifting through the trash barrels at the end of each week and grabbing what appeared to be usable parts.

Calling the scavenged hardware "usable" was about as far from the truth as it could be. There was something wrong with each part, enough that it had been rejected by plant inspectors. Most of the rejects were switches, each of which was potentially dangerous.

The hardware in the crate marked with blue was supposed to be stuff that Sparky had purchased from local hardware dealers or nascent electrical supply houses. He used that hardware for the working-class homes and the *gratis* installations that he arranged out of the goodness of his heart. Sparky didn't know of the avalanche in the back of the truck on their journey from Chambersburg, nor that Mikey had unwittingly commingled the hardware from the two crates when he cleaned up the mess.

As they were preparing to leave George Ruth's saloon one morning and head to Ruxton to wire up yet another summer home, they stopped by Willie's house on Division Street to follow up on their installation. Sparky also went next door to the Marshall home and saw that Mrs. Marshall had delivered a healthy baby boy that they had named "Thoroughgood," after a great-grandfather.

Everything in the immaculate Washington and Marshall homes was working as it should, so Sparky and his team drove north to Ruxton Heights, arriving at their new job site just before lunch. It took most of the afternoon for them to survey the property and to establish the wiring paths for the electrical service. Sparky worked with the construction foreman to mark the electrical service on the blueprints for the stately home and prepared a list of the equipment they would need to complete the job.

For this particular summer home, the owner would not be on site during construction. Sparky was glad that he and his team, and especially Willie, would not be under constant surveillance on the job site. They would be left alone to do their work in coordination with the instructions of the site foreman. Sparky estimated that wiring the house while it was still bare studs would take a matter of three days.

Back on Division Street, Charity Washington was getting her younger sister Velma situated in a small room that had once been a study. The room was too small to be of use as a permanent bedroom, but Velma was only planning on staying for a week or two while she was waiting for her husband to come north from Virginia to find work. During the day, the small room had plenty of natural light as it was windowed on three sides. After dark, a single bulb in a ceiling fixture just recently installed by Sparky would provide illumination.

Charity and Velma spent the early evening catching up on family gossip. They talked about almost-forgotten cousins, grandparents who were born in slavery, and how life just wasn't fair to black folk. After supper, Velma felt she needed to retire for the evening and wanted to spend some time reading her Bible before bed.

It wasn't long after Velma climbed the stairs to her room that Charity noticed the lights dim for a few moments. Charity was puzzled. The dimming was usually followed by a fuse blowing, which Sparky had already taught her how to replace. This was different: the lights dimmed and then returned to full brightness. Once the lights were fully bright again, Charity heard a loud thud upstairs.

Thinking that one of the children had fallen out of bed, Charity flew up the stairs two at a time. When she reached the top step, the acrid smell of burned flesh and hair assaulted her nostrils. "Could a rat have chewed through the wiring?" she wondered. Charity then checked on the children and found them sound asleep in their beds. Next was Velma's room, where Charity called out, "Velma? Are you okay?" There was no answer.

Charity reached inside the room to find the light switch. Pressing the top button should have turned on the overhead light, but instead all Charity got was a clicking sound. She took one more careful step in the near-darkness and tripped over her sister's prostrate form.

Charity, who had worked briefly in a segregated medical clinic before she was pregnant with her first child, quickly knelt by her sister's side and checked for a pulse. There was none. Stifling a scream, Charity ran down the stairs, out the front door, and to the Marshall's front door, where she began banging furiously. "Mrs. Marshall? Help me, please! I think my sister is dead."

Norma Marshall handled the situation just like she did an unruly classroom. She was all business and calm under pressure. She, too, checked Velma's pulse – and felt a very faint, almost imperceptible flutter of a heartbeat. Though she had no formal medical training, her duties as a teacher required that she at least be aware of basic triage for injuries and checking a person's pulse was one of the steps.

"Charity, run to my house and telephone the doctor. Tell him it is an emergency. He might still be able to save your sister, but it seems that she has been badly shocked."

"Yes'm…" Charity mumbled and was on her way to the Marshall foyer where the telephone was installed.

Samuel Gold, M.D., a white man, took his time arriving. He was being called away from a family dinner and, despite Charity's assertion of emergency, felt that it probably was too late to help the patient anyway. He had seen more than his share of electrocutions and they usually did not end well for the victim.

The doctor's assessment was, unfortunately, quite accurate. The next morning, the *Baltimore Sun* carried a short announcement in the page facing the obituaries:

"A Negro woman, Velma Smith, was electrocuted yesterday in the Division Street home of her sister, Mrs. Charity Washington. Foul play is not suspected as the Washington home was recently electrified. A local teacher, Mrs. Norma Marshall, administered aid, but was not successful in reviving Miss Smith, who was pronounced dead at the scene by Doctor Samuel Gold."

Chapter Thirteen: Detective Work
Spring, 1908

Doctor Robert Mittford had taken Sean Mulcahy's threats seriously and not pursued Edgar Allan Butler's cause of death any further. Instead, Mittford focused his energies on other electrocutions in Allentown, Harrisburg, and now Baltimore. Mittford did not like being threatened by the likes of Sean Mulcahy, regardless of who he worked for, and decided to retire from active medical practice to take up his investigations full-time. Unfortunately, he had to move from Allentown to keep from running even further afoul ot Mulcahy and his boss, Waldo Emerson Butler.

After some back-and-forth correspondence and a couple of telegrams, Mittford was invited by his friend, Henry Mills Hurd, M.D., to take a sabbatical in Baltimore and use The Johns Hopkins Hospital as his research base. Mittford readily accepted the offer and was provided with a small medical resident's apartment on hospital grounds. Though meager, the apartment provided Mittford with everything he needed: a bed and a private bathroom with a flush toilet and bathtub. With a letter from Dr. Hurd, Robert Mittford was allowed to take his meals in the hospital's staff cafeteria and had privileges in the hospital morgue and laboratories.

Baltimore had recently been added to his list because of the 1905 electrocutions at the summer homes of some of the wealthy escaping the Baltimore heat. As he had already discovered, the common thread connecting the electrocutions was the family's wealth and their summer home's proximity to a rail line.

Mittford was puzzled, however, that there were no working-class electrocutions mentioned in any of the newspapers – except for the death of Miss Velma Smith in Baltimore. Were the working-class and Negro deaths not reported, or were they happening at a far lower rate than those of the wealthy? Mittford wanted answers, even if he had to read every newspaper that had been published in the past ten years.

The tiny apartment Mittford occupied was quickly filled with journals and copies of newspapers. He subscribed to the *Baltimore Sun* and had the daily papers from Allentown and Harrisburg delivered as well. Unless the papers contained some mention of electricity, electrification, or electrocutions, they were thrown away. Mittford only kept the relevant editions, including those that contained information on electric chair electrocutions. If his keywords did not appear as he scanned the text, the entire newspaper was put in the trash. Subscribing to three dailies would quickly fill his meager accommodations, leaving room for little else.

After about a week in residence, Mittford read an obituary in the Harrisburg paper:

Henry Langston Dead of Electrocution

The article went on to describe Langston as one of the wealthiest men in the Chambersburg area and a close associate of J. T. Chalmers. Mittford raised his left eyebrow as he read and jotted down notes in his journal. Once again, it was a wealthy family that was affected. The one thing that was missing from the equation was proximity to a rail line: Langston's summer home was about as far away from the Cumberland Valley Railroad line as it could be and only reachable by horse-drawn carriage or motorcar.

Reading the news about Langston, Mittford had an epiphany: he needed to add the Chambersburg or Hagerstown daily newspaper to his subscriptions. Because the latter was in Maryland and on a direct daily rail line to Baltimore, he would receive papers from Hagerstown quicker than from Chambersburg. He needed the information quickly, not weeks or months after an incident; the papers usually reached the Enoch Pratt Free Library on overnight trains within two days of publication.

Each mention of an incident involving electricity was logged in Mittford's handwritten journal. The date, location, and name of the involved party were all recorded, as was the source and any other amplifying information. It didn't take more than a couple of weeks before Mittford began to see a trend.

Mittford recognized that most of the "accidental" deaths occurred at locations which had just recently received electrical service. His records, as far back as 1905, seemed to support this hypothesis. The unanswered question was "Why?" Were the victims specifically targeted? Did they have anything in common? His list now included Velma Smith and Henry Langston; their social circles were as unlikely to mix as oil and water.

Initially, Mittford thought that wealthy families were being targeted in some way. He could not explain the coincidence of Henry Langston and Velma Smith. Their deaths were separated by just a few days, but in two locations that were over eighty miles apart.

Mittford decided that he needed to consult with an electricity expert, perhaps one of the men who had been installing electrical hardware in and around The Johns Hopkins Hospital. Mittford got permission from the administrator, Dr. Hurd, to reach out to the hospital's chief electrician and maintenance supervisor, Albert Greenlaw. Most people called him "Albie," in private, but the doctors and nurses insisted on more formal terms of address, at least while they were all at work. He was "Mr. Greenlaw" in those circles.

"Mr. Greenlaw, can you explain to me how switches work?" Dr. Mittford inquired during his first meeting with the tradesman.

"A switch is a simple device, Dr. Mittford," Greenlaw replied. "It closes a circuit between the source and destination. Pretty simple, really."

"Could someone intentionally tamper with a switch and render it dangerous?" Mittford asked.

"Anything's possible, I reckon. It's not likely, though. Somebody would have to know about the inner workings of a switch," Greenlaw answered.

"Of course... but that person would not have to have an extensive background or training in electricity?" Mittford asked rhetorically; he already knew what the answer would be.

"Like I already told you, switches are child's play, Dr. Mittford. It doesn't take any special skill to take one apart and tamper with its innards." Greenlaw was getting annoyed with Mittford's almost lawyerly inquest.

"Can you show me the inner workings, the innards – as you say, of a switch?" Mittford's interest had been piqued by Greenlaw's last reply.

"Certainly, Dr. Mittford. Give me five minutes to find a decent example." Mittford could sense Greenlaw's unease at being questioned.

Heading at a snail's pace through the door to the workshop adjoining his cubicle of an office, Albie Greenlaw was muttering to himself about the inconvenience of "another know-it-all doctor" being nosy. He wanted Mittford to go away and let him get about his work. It seemed, Greenlaw thought, that "every time I deal with one of them doctors, trouble ain't far behind."

Mittford could hear Greenlaw moving items around in his workshop. Greenlaw certainly was not quiet and Mittford wondered if the noise was to emphasize how much Greenlaw felt he was annoyed and being inconvenienced. It was obvious to Mittford that Greenlaw was stalling more than he was interested in helping.

Albie Greenlaw's hermitage was the bowels of the hospital. Rarely seeing the light of day, he had no family and no emotional attachment to anyone, except perhaps the old coal-fired boiler he called "Medusa." He kept a cot in the boiler room and bathed in the locker room reserved for the janitorial workforce. Mittford had seen Greenlaw's type before, most of whom eventually ended up committing heinous crimes or in straitjackets at the insane asylum. Mittford wondered how long it would take before Greenlaw fit into either category.

After what seemed like an eternity, Greenlaw emerged from the workshop with a box full of switches. "Is this what you are looking for, Doctor?"

'Yes, it is. Can you show me how they work, please?" Mittford asked.

Greenlaw inhaled deeply, then exhaled heavily in feigned exasperation. He was annoyed, for sure, but that was because every time Dr. Mittford asked for something, it was extending the time Greenlaw was having to deal with another person. Albie Greenlaw certainly was not a social animal and did not suffer idle chit-chat.

"Watch me carefully, Doctor..." Greenlaw replied, taking the switch in his left hand and a Robertson driver in his right. Use of the just-patented Robertson head screw was spreading throughout component producers, with Edison's General Electric Company being one of the early adopters. Switch housings were fastened together with the Robertson screw, which helped reduce or eliminate stripped heads and cracked housings that were the result of over-torquing.

Greenlaw turned the screws counterclockwise and loosened them to separate the two halves of the switch housing. The half remaining in his left hand contained all of the inner workings; the right half of the housing was empty; Greenlaw set it down on the desk between himself and Dr. Mittford.

"This part here," Greenlaw said, trying to sound as learned as he could," engages between the contacts to complete a circuit. Until the switch is thrown, no 'lectricity can get through… Unless there is a metal fragment or wire trimming that crosses the gap between the contacts."

"Could someone intentionally cause that?" Mittford queried.

"They could, but why would anyone want to?" Greenlaw countered.

Mittford fell silent and did not reply to Greenlaw's rhetorical question. Instead, he changed his line of questioning. "Mr. Greenlaw, how would someone receive an electrical shock from a switch?"

Greenlaw suddenly realized that he actually knew more than a learned doctor. "That, Dr. Mittford, is easy to explain. Someone with know-how and the right tools could bridge the hot side of the switch to the coverplate. That would electrify the plate and cause electricity to pass through a person's body to a grounding point. We call that a 'ground fault.' It doesn't happen very often, but when it does, the person getting shocked is usually dead before they hit the floor." Mittford's face was devoid of emotion.

"Mr. Greenlaw, I thank you for your time. Good day to you, sir." Mittford turned on his heels and headed for the nearest stairway that would take him back above ground to the light of day.

Returning to his meager accommodation, Mittford wrote his notes from memory. As had been his custom during his decades-long career as a physician, Mittford always compiled his notes after-the-fact so he could focus on his patient. He applied the same technique to the investigative work he was currently engaged in.

By relying on his own memory, he did not unduly influence the subject's contributions. One of his early mentors emphasized that diligent notetaking often allowed the patient to think something was important at the time. The reality, from a clinical standpoint, was often completely different.

Over the next hour, Mittford wrote everything he could remember about his encounter with Greenlaw. Reaching the end of his memories, Mittford wrote, "intentional modification and sabotage of switches is possible."

Chapter Fourteen: Going Deep
Summer, 1908

The more Robert Mittford dug into the electrocutions, the more confused he became. He had evidence of nearly one hundred deaths since the turn of the century. Most of the deaths were among the wealthiest segments of the population. At first, Mittford thought they were being targeted and his reasoning was biased in that direction.

Mittford timelined the electrification of Allentown, Harrisburg, Chambersburg, and Baltimore. As he analyzed the information, he suddenly realized that the wealthy would be the ones who could afford to have their homes and businesses electrified ahead of most of the population. Therefore, he deduced, it was most likely for the incidence of electrocutions to disproportionately affect the wealthy.

The outliers were cases like those of Miss Velma Smith in Baltimore. It seemed like electrocutions in the working class or black neighborhoods were only reported in the newspapers when there was space that had not been taken up by other news or society events. A wealthy victim would get a full-page column, but a factory worker would get a meager sentence or two, even less if the victim was from a "colored neigbhorhood." The Baltimore Sun's announcement of Miss Velma Smith's demise was, Mittford determined, unusually long. "Perhaps it was because the informant, Mrs. Marshall, was a well-respected colored schoolteacher. Her profession gave her more credibility than an unskilled laborer," Mittford thought to himself.

Dr. Robert Mittford was no wallflower. He was engaging and loquacious – except when he was anywhere near Sean Mulcahy. He quickly decided it was worth a trip to Division Street to interview Mrs. Marshall and see what might have transpired with her next-door neighbor's sister. He just hoped that Mrs. Marshall would be willing to talk to a white man about the incident.

The next morning, Mittford made his way to Division Street on a cross-town trolley car from his dormitory at The Johns Hopkins Hospital. Baltimore's transit system at the time was very efficient. It was the first city to provide electrified trolley service, with the first cars in operation during the late 1880s. Mittford marveled at the ingenuity of the inventors and how they had harnessed electricity.

City schools were already dismissed for the summer and he found Mrs. Marshall sitting on the spotless marble stoop outside her home, gently bouncing a fussy infant on her knee. "Shhh… Thoroughgood… Mama's here…"

After introductions, Mrs. Marshall was cordial, but wary of a white man asking questions about a death that had taken place just a few yards from where they stood. "Dr. Mittford, you have to understand that it is highly unusual for a white man to be asking questions around here. It's usually the police…"

"Mrs. Marshall, thank you for your candor. I truly appreciate your openness," he replied. "I am investigating deaths by electrocution to see if there is a common causative factor. There have been deaths here in Baltimore, as well as in Pennsylvania… Allentown, Harrisburg, and Chambersburg, to be precise."

"Why is Velma Smith's death of such interest to you, Dr. Mittford? She was just a poor black woman down on her luck and visiting her sister," Mrs. Marshall said quizzically as she cocked her head and raised an eyebrow. "When the police and coroner left, I heard them say, 'just another dead nigger,' and I bit my tongue knowing they were not going to do anything at all on this case, even if it was an accident. Velma's death deserved just as much respect as a rich white woman's from Ruxton or Lawyers Hill." Mrs. Marshall's tone was icy and her gaze stern.

Mittford paused for a moment to allow a silence to calm Mrs. Marshall. "I spent most of yesterday talking to an electrician at the hospital. He explained to me that it was possible for someone to tamper with a switch and cause it to short-circuit," he explained.

"Dr. Mittford, are you trying to tell me that Velma's death was no accident?" Norma Marshall asked.

"It's too soon to tell. I don't have a lot to go on… just a hunch at the moment," Mittford replied. "Could you arrange for me to speak with Mrs. Washington?"

"Of course, Dr. Mittford. It would be my pleasure to make the introductions," Norma Marshall beamed. Mittford was a white man she instinctively trusted and having him speak to her neighbor was the right thing to do. There were some things about Velma's death that were unnerving. After all, her own brother-in-law was involved in wiring the two homes for electricity. If nothing else, Willie's name – and that of his white employer – would be clear. Rumors were already running rampant around Division Street that there was some foul play involved. "Why should we trust a white man?" seemed to be a common thread.

As Mrs. Marshall expected, the police had not investigated Velma Smith's death at all, instead relying on the perfunctory input of the Baltimore City Coroner to decide if foul play had been involved. The official ruling was "accidental death, presumably by electrocution." That ended any possibility of a police investigation.

After making introductions, Mrs. Marshall left Charity Washington alone with Dr. Mittford on their front stoop. They sat together, discussing Velma's demise, drawing side-eye glances from the passers-by, all of whom were black. Mittford knew he was out of place in that neighborhood and could sense that he was being watched from every possible angle and not just by the pedestrians on the sidewalk.

Dabbing at tears with a spotless linen handkerchief, Charity told her sister's story, about how she had been down on her luck and nearly destitute. Velma had been cast aside by a man twice her age when she physically resisted his sexual advances. She had shown up on Charity's doorstep quite unexpectedly, walking nearly the entire 35-mile distance from Washington, D.C. Hungry and in desperate need of a bath, Velma went to the only place she knew she would be safe: her sister's home in Baltimore.

Velma had been in Baltimore just over a week before she was electrocuted. Charity told Mittford that, for the first three nights in the Washington home, Velma would wake in the middle of the night, screaming in terror. "Each night," she would tell her sister, "it's the same dream. That man comin' after me after I kicked him... *there*..." Velma was too embarrassed to provide more specific details. The choice of words and a downward nod of her head was enough for Charity to understand. My sister said, "Charity, he was howling like a hurt hound dog and sayin' he was gonna kill me... so I kicked him again... that stopped him dead in his tracks. Oh, the sounds comin' out of that man's mouth! They's almost not even human!"

"Are these your sister's words, Mrs. Washington?" Mittford asked.

"Yes, Dr. Mittford. I remember them plain as day," Charity replied. "Our momma didn't raise us to be liars."

"May I take a look at the room where Velma... you know..." Mittford asked as his voice wavered.

"Follow me, please, Dr. Mittford," Charity said in a voice just above a whisper. She had, up to now, been able to avoid going back into her sister's room once the body had been taken away. Now, with Dr. Mittford investigating, a return to that room could no longer be avoided.

Charity Washington motioned for Mittford to go into the room while she stood outside wiping her cheeks with the linen handkerchief. Mittford sketched the layout of the room, raising his left eyebrow as he took his notes. Overall, the setting was "unremarkable," except for a star-like burn mark around the room's only light switch. It was consistent with the image of a short circuit that Greenlaw had described the day before.

"Mrs. Washington, had your sister just gotten out of a bath or perhaps had been soaked to the skin by a rain storm?" Mittford asked.

"She had just gotten out of a bath, I think," Charity replied.

"Was anyone else home at the time?" Mittford inquired.

"I was here, doing some mending. I heard a popping sound and then a thud… that must have been when Velma hit the floor," Charity said softly.

"Did your husband or his boss replace the lightswitch after Velma's demise?" Mittford asked.

"Mr. Thompson is going to teach Willie, that's my husband, how to replace light switches and this is the one they are starting with," Charity said with noticeable pride in her voice. *"My husband is more than just a laborer,"* she thought to herself.

"Mrs. Washington, do you have access to a telephone?" Mittford needed to be sure she could contact him when it was time to replace the switch.

"Yes, sir. Mrs. Marshall said I could use their telephone any time," Charity answered.

"When Mr. Thompson is here to replace that switch, I would appreciate it if you could give me a call. The hospital's answering service will take a message for me if I am not there," Mittford instructed.

"Of course, Dr. Mittford. You have a good day, now!"

"Thank you, Mrs. Washington. I will be in touch."

As Mittford walked away, he was even more confused than before. If Mr. Thompson was willing to come back and replace the switch *and* use it as a teaching tool for his apprentice, it was highly unlikely that there was any intentional foul play. Mittford had to get his hands on the switch that was in place when Velma Smith died.

Chapter Fifteen: Switches
Mid-Summer, 1908

Less than a week after Mittford had his first meetings with Norma Marshall and Charity Washington, he received a message from the Hopkins answering service: "Mrs. Washington requests your presence at her home. You know the address." Mittford wondered if this was the call he had been waiting for, where the electrician would be replacing the switch in Velma Washington's temporary bedroom.

Mittford immediately went down to the bowels of the hospital and sought out the building superintendent and head electrician, Albert Greenlaw, once more. *"It might be beneficial to take Mr. Greenlaw with me to Division Street,"* Mittford thought to himself.

Knocking on the door to Greenlaw's basement hermitage before entering, Mittford called out, "Mr. Greenlaw? Are you here?" The only sounds Doctor Mittford heard was the hissing of the boiler that Greenlaw called "Medusa" and the popping of a clinker being formed. Mittford went deeper into the bowels of the steam works, hoping to find Greenlaw engaged in some repair or another and perhaps beyond earshot.

Rounding a corner in the labyrinth of passageways beneath the main hospital, Mittford was met with the acrid odor of burned flesh, which he instantly recognized as burned *human* flesh. Not since his medical school days had he encountered it so intensely. It was so distasteful and nauseating that Mittford had to use his breast pocket handkerchief to cover his nose and mouth as bile rose in his throat.

Mittford remembered enough of his previous meeting with Greenlaw to know that the electrical service panel was not far away. All of the wiring led to the panel. One more corner and he would be there...

The next thing Mittford saw was even more upsetting than the acrid smell: Greenlaw with his arms outstretched between two switches, scorched to a crisp. Smoke was still rising from his singed hair and clothing. Mittford also knew that there could be live electricity coursing through Greenlaw's remains.

Finding a wooden pole, Mittford pried Greenlaw's hands from the two switches; the body crumpled to the floor, arms breaking into pieces like an overcooked whole chicken. Mittford vomited and then regained his composure. There was a house telephone back at

Greenlaw's official desk, and Mittford needed to inform someone, perhaps his friend, Dr. Hurd, that there had been an accident in the hospital basement.

Also on Greenlaw's desk was an outside phone, connected to the local exchange, where Mittford could call Mrs. Marshall and inform her of the delay. He did so without providing a specific reason beyond "something has intervened and I am not presently available."

Once Dr. Hurd arrived, he asked Mittford to contact an electrician to ascertain if there had been any damage to the hospital's wiring. The only electrician that Mittford knew of was the one who had wired the Marshall and Washington homes; he immediately rang Mrs. Marshall again and asked that she dispatch Mr. Thompson and her husband to the hospital without delay.

Once at the hospital, Sparky and Willie were escorted to the labyrinthine basement. Dr. Mittford and Dr. Hurd met them at the entrance to Greenlaw's little empire and escorted them to the scene of Greenlaw's demise. Sparky could tell immediately that Greenlaw had touched the two switches simultaneously, one being switched on and the other being switched off, and enabled his body to bridge between the two switches – along with the full current of electricity.

Sparky traced the electrical lines back to the fuse panel. "Dr. Hurd, I need your permission to disable this circuit. I do not know where it goes, but in order to investigate the cause of Mr. Greenlaw's accident, I have to remove the switches for examination."

"Of course, Mr. Thompson, you have my approval. Just be quick about it," Hurd replied.

"Once the live electricity is shut off, I can remove the two switches and tie their wires together. This will force whatever they were switching to remain in an 'always-on' state," Sparky explained. He could tell from experience that Dr. Hurd was yet another person who could not fathom the workings of electricity; the look of disinterest and boredom on Hurd's face confirmed Sparky's suspicion.

Switches removed and power restored, Sparky took the two switches to the work table in Greenlaw's shop. A few minutes later, Sparky had the switches open and was examining them.

"Hmm…" Sparky said as he stroked his chin absent-mindedly, "this is very interesting. It appears that both of these switches were faulty from the start and it was only a matter of time before someone got shocked."

Mittford furrowed his brow and cocked his head. What he was hearing was perplexing: could it be that the string of electrocutions in Maryland and Pennsylvania were attributable to faulty components? Mittford's energy was renewed by this breakthrough.

"Mr. Thompson... Sparky... Why are such switches being sold to contractors such as yourself? Mittford asked.

"We place our orders directly to Mr. Edison's company and trust that they will be filled in a timely manner. They usually are... but when they can't be filled quickly, I have a contact inside the company who sells me certain components at a cost much lower than buying directly from Edison's salespeople."

"Interesting," Mittford commented. "Who is the person you contact for your switches?"

"His name is John Garfield. He was my only friend when I worked at the Edison factories. John was always good for a laugh, and a prankster, too!"

At that precise moment, there was a knock on the workshop door. "Police. Open up, please."

"Henry, what did you do?" Mittford asked.

"I had to call the police – and the coroner – to report Greenlaw's demise. Even if it was accidental, the police need to compile a report," Hurd responded.

"But… but… they won't do as thorough an investigation as I will," Mittford said, *sotto voce.* "You should hear how they handled the electrocution of a colored lady, Mr. Washington's sister-in-law, up on Division Street.

Moving out of earshot of the police officers, Hurd said quite sternly, "Robert, you can certainly continue your research and try to tie Greenlaw's unfortunate end to whatever it is you are investigating – but you are not to interfere with the police in any way. I remind you, sir, that you are being accommodated at the hospital on my good graces, a situation that could be terminated at a moment's notice."

"Of course, my friend. I understand," Mittford hung his head as he replied. He knew that neither Velma Washington's death nor Albie Greenlaw's gruesome demise would get the attention they deserved from the Baltimore Police Department. Greenlaw was a loner who shunned most external contact and Velma Washington was a Negro from out of town. Mittford knew they deserved the same attention as wealthy families, but realized that there was little chance of equitable treatment. They were gone and would not be missed except by their immediate families.

Mittford and Hurd stepped back to observe Sparky Thompson's exchange with the police officers. It was becoming more and more animated as Sparky explained the manner in which he procured his components. The police were, from their actions and tone, suggesting that there was some foul play involved and that Sparky was the likely culprit.

"I did not do anything to cause their deaths!" Sparky said, his voice almost in a panicked scream. "I was taught by Mr. Edison himself and would never do anything to intentionally cause harm to another human being. Electricity can be dangerous and I go to great lengths to ensure everything is safe before I leave. I even teach the homeowner and their servants, if they have them, how things work and what could go wrong if water and electricity are too close together."

"Mr. Thompson, you need to come with us down to the station," the burly police sergeant said gruffly.

"Am I under arrest?"

"No, Mr. Thompson, we just want to ask you some more questions," the sergeant responded.

As they left, Sparky pleaded with Mittford to contact his apprentices, Seamus and Willie, as soon as he could and let them know what had just happened. Mittford obliged and headed immediately to the Washington home on Division Street. Willie in turn headed to George Ruth's saloon and rooming house to find Seamus. Moving through the segregated neighborhoods between Division Street and Conway Street, Willie was careful to be deferential and not make direct eye contact with any of the white people – and especially not with any white women. He had heard of colored men, including teen-aged boys, being beaten and even lynched for the most trivial contact with white women.

Reaching Seamus's room, Willie told him the news. "Mr. Sparky's been taken by the police. They think he had something to do with our Velma's death and some guy that works at that big hospital."

Seamus knew from rumors what was in store for Sparky once he reached the police precinct house. He would be grilled for hours without a break, denied even the most basic of comforts, and eventually threatened with physical violence – all with the aim of coercing a confession. He was truly worried for his boss's safety.

"Willie, you go back home and tend to your family. I will handle this. I know the police won't take kindly to a colored fella like you showing up on their doorstep and demanding that a white man be released. You'd be setting yourself up for a beating," Seamus explained.

As Seamus headed for the police station, Dr. Robert Mittford returned to his dormitory room and began poring over the newspapers once again. *"There has to be something in common between all of these accidental electrocutions,"* he thought to himself. For the next several hours, he examined and re-examined the stacks of papers and eventually dozed off.

Mittford's vivid dreams took him back to the bowels of the hospital and the conversation with Sparky Thompson: the switches were faulty and they came directly from the Edison factory. He woke with a start and, after allowing a few moments for his head to clear, realized that his dreams were pointing him in a direction he had not previously considered: the Edison factory complex in New Jersey.

Chapter Sixteen: New Jersey
Late Summer, 1908

After the death of Velma Smith in Baltimore, Sparky had mentioned his friend from West Orange, John Garfield. Could it be that Garfield was the culprit selling defective components? Mittford would have expected that Sparky's friends were totally above-board, like Sparky, and incorruptible.

Dr. Mittford decided early the next morning that he would have to go to New Jersey and investigate the source of the components that Sparky Thompson was using. Sparky, Mittford had determined, was the common denominator for all but a couple of the electrocutions Mittford had read about in the newspapers across Maryland and Pennsylvania. There was no way they were coincidental. Mittford just had to prove it.

Mittford did not know of any medical colleagues living or working in the West Orange area; the closest was at the New Jersey Home for Disabled Soldiers, Sailors or Marines in Vineland – over 100 miles away. He would be on his own for lodging and board, unless he could convince a local doctor to sponsor him for privileges at the Orange

Memorial Hospital. Such things took time in 1908. There were letters to be exchanged, references to be contacted, and projects to be defined. The mail was slow and there was only so much information that could be exchanged via telegram. The entire process could take weeks, weeks that Mittford could not spare.

Discretion was also necessary: Edison's General Electric Corporation was well-respected in West Orange but not known for its philanthropy, except to fund other inventors' research. The community at large reaped little benefit – other than employment – from Thomas Alva Edison. Turning to Edison's beneficiaries could backfire: none were likely to be frank with an interloper like Mittford.

Robert Mittford accepted the risks of digging deep into Edison and his company. He had to get to the bottom of the mysterious electrocutions. His hypothesis was that someone was selling defective components that should have been destroyed. He just had to prove it.

Before Dr. Robert Mittford could begin any of his detective work, he had to worry about lodging. West Orange was not known for palatial accommodations, with most visitors preferring upscale accommodations in either Newark or New York City. Mittford knew he needed to be close to or in West Orange to not appear as a "city feller" interloper. In the end, he was allowed a room at the Essex Country Club after unexpectedly running into a colleague from medical school who was a member there.

Mittford's assimilation into the community was nearly immediate, once residents found out he was a doctor used to dealing with the health issues of the wealthy and the discretion those dealings required. It was almost an unfortunate circumstance of his presence and a distraction from the true reason of his visit to West Orange. He finally had to insist that medical issues be brought to him between 9 a.m. and noon just so he could have his afternoons free to carry out his investigation. The vestibule to the men's locker room was Mittford's waiting room.

Country clubs were the bastion of male recreation in the early decades of the 20th Century. Ladies were tolerated and not generally welcome outside of the dining room or public social areas. It was because of his discretion that Dr. Robert Mittford was able to treat all sorts of male maladies, especially those that resulted from dalliances with women outside the marriage bed. Fortunately for Mittford and his patients, the Wasserman test had been developed just a couple of years earlier, but it was not always accurate for early infections. Mittford knew this and advised his patients accordingly.

The first week of seeing patients was complete and Mittford was ready to begin his investigation. Using the newly compiled city telephone directory as his primary resource, he was able to determine that there were only two John Garfields in West Orange. It was customary for city telephone directories of the day to include employment or professional information. The first John Garfield was listed as "atty" for attorney. The second was listed with his place of employment, "GenElec," and an address of 272 ½ Snyder Street.

The "½" in the address meant that the occupant probably was renting out an upstairs or loft space from the owner. That, Mittford knew, usually indicated a person down on their luck. Garfield's position at the Edison complex was low level; he was a member of the janitorial staff and had no real responsibilities.

Snyder Street had seen better days. The once well-maintained homes were falling into disrepair. The street, even with its intricate brickwork, was potholed; many of the newfangled automobiles suffered flat tires as a result.

The sewer system was also suspect as the odor of raw human waste permeated the area after heavy rains.

The one saving grace of Snyder Street was that there were benches every few yards. Mittford noticed this and decided that he could inconspicuously watch Number 272 and learn more about the habits of the mysterious John Garfield. The trick would be to gradually increase his time on the benches so that passers-by would not take any notice of the man who seemed to have become a permanent fixture on the benches. Mittford knew it might take a week, maybe more, before people greeted him out of familiarity.

During his first short stay on Snyder Street, Mittford saw John Garfield leaving 272½ around noon and mounting a bicycle. The timing was such that Mittford believed Garfield was returning to the Edison complex after his lunch break. It was reasonable, with the distance of barely a mile between the two locations, that Garfield could make it home and back again in less than an hour.

One thing that Dr. Mittford could not immediately ascertain was quitting time at the Edison facility. Rumors abounded that Edison himself supervised daily operations and ruled the shop floor with a tyrannical passion. The men never knew from one day to the next when they might be released for the evening – and there were no unions to negotiate or enforce daily hours of work.

Like most industrial complexes of the early 1900s, Edison's General Electric facilities had a steam whistle that would signal the start and end of work periods. It blew every morning at 7 a.m. sharp, again when the men were released for lunch, a third time when there were five minutes left in the meal period, and a final time to mark the end of the work day. Mittford quickly determined that the fourth whistle never sounded at the same time two days in a row.

Mittford had heard the "end of meal period" whistle. He looked at his pocket watch: it was about ten minutes after John Garfield mounted his bicycle and headed for the Edison complex. Knowing that it was unlikely for Garfield to return home before the end of the workday, Mittford headed for the nearest diner to get something to eat.

Frank's Diner was just a couple of blocks away. Mittford had heard that the food there was quite palatable, depending on the day of the week and the special being served. Regardless of the special, there was always fresh pie and the coffee was definitely among the best in town.

The presentation and ambience were certainly a step down from the country club, but at least he would not be bothered by members seeking medical advice. There was an enjoyable anonymity at the diner, and it was not unusual to see men enjoying a solitary meal in the middle of the day. Aside from the counter girl taking his order and refilling his coffee cup, there were no other opportunities for Mittford to engage in conversation.

Sitting on a stool at the counter, Mittford was quickly lost in his own thoughts. Something was causing the "accidental" electrocutions. Something or someone. He just could not put a cohesive line of reasoning together. The only consistency was that the devices came from Edison's General Electric company.

Mittford took out his notebook to record his thoughts but was quickly sidetracked by a conversation between the two men seated a few stools away. They were not making any effort to speak in hushed tones. Mittford did his best to look absorbed in his own thoughts and began doodling absent-mindedly in his notebook.

"I tell ya, it's scary," one of the men said, "Garfield takes the spoils from the trash pile and does God-knows-what with it all."

"He's just a janitor. What good would the stuff be to him without any knowledge of what he was taking?" the other man asked.

"Well, he was good friends with that Thompson guy… I think his first name was Archibald or something like that. You know… the one who was always pulling pranks. I think he was dismissed, but I am not sure. It's been a few years since he left," the first man explained.

The men never said it precisely, but Mittford now had evidence, albeit hearsay, that John Garfield was involved in something nefarious and had connected an unwitting Sparky Thompson to the scheme. Mittford wanted to know more about what the two men were discussing and even considered joining their conversation somehow. Instead, he decided to sit by and listen; joining the conversation would be more awkward than simply remaining quiet.

The overheard diner conversation also jogged Mittford's memory. He was instantly taken back to the last conversation he had with Sean Mulcahy, Waldo Emerson Butler's private security force of one. Something was amiss. He thought that Butler had been behind his own son's death simply to collect the double indemnity life insurance. Now he wasn't so sure that was the truth. Sure,

Butler probably wanted the instant cash that would result from his son's demise – but would Butler have actually been brazen enough to cause it? Perhaps it was simply a death of convenience that benefitted Waldo Emerson Butler and his nearly bankrupt railroad empire.

Chapter Seventeen: Mittford's Decision
New Jersey and Pennsylvania, Autumn, 1908

As summer turned to fall and the leaves began to display their vivid fall hues, Doctor Robert Mittford was invited to stay on permanently at the Essex Country Club as their physician-in-residence. The terms of the offer included free room and board in return for medical advice to its more affluent (and privacy-conscious) members. The Club also agreed to pay for Mittford's numerous newspaper subscriptions and to provide a significant cash stipend for his discretionary spending.

Contemplating the generous offer, he could not help but think that leaving Allentown was proving to be quite lucrative; he would just have to return there one more time to close up his practice and take down his shingle. The practice had been idle for several months already. Mrs. Hanscom had already resigned and there were no other entanglements or attachments to Allentown... except for Waldo Emerson Butler and Sean Mulcahy.

On the train back to Allentown from West Orange, Mittford had plenty of time to think. He decided that it would be best to confront Emerson directly about his son's demise, hopefully without any involvement from Mulcahy. It had been over a year since Edgar Allan Butler's "accidental" demise. The elder Butler had already received the life insurance payment and rescued his railroad empire from financial ruin. Mittford believed that the tenor of the situation had changed dramatically since their last encounter.

Once back in Allentown, Mittford headed for the gentleman's social club and a quick meal. There, he found Butler at his usual table, where Butler was uncharacteristically jovial and welcoming. In fact, Mittford was invited to join Butler for lunch.

A quick scan of the room revealed that Sean Mulcahy was nowhere to be seen. Mittford was puzzled. He thought the two men were as thick as thieves several months earlier, to the extent that Mulcahy appeared ready to commit all manner of crimes at the behest of his employer.

"Doctor Mittford, it is a pleasure to see you once again. I was afraid you were never returning to our fair city," Butler said jovially.

"Waldo, I am going to be in Allentown just long enough to shut down my practice, pack up my equipment, and return to New Jersey. I have been offered a lucrative position there that will keep me employed and housed for the foreseeable future. Have you ever heard of the Essex Country Club?" Mittford asked.

"Yes, of course! It is one of the most exclusive clubs in New Jersey. In fact, I think it is actually the oldest golf course in that state," Butler replied.

"The situation they have offered me is one that will not put the demands on my time that a private practice does. I will be treating mainly the male members of the club – women are allowed on weekends, and then only in the dining rooms. I shall be able to continue my research into what is causing the electrocutions…"

Butler interrupted, "Like what happened to my son? His death was accidental. That was the coroner's ruling and I shall not discuss the matter any further."

"Waldo, listen to me… his death may have been accidental, but its proximate cause appears to have been defective equipment somehow removed from Thomas Edison's General Electric complex in West Orange," Mittford countered.

"What are you trying to tell me, Mittford?"

"Edgar's electrocution was not merely an accident. It was because of faulty hardware that I believe was intentionally removed from Edison's factory and sold for a handsome profit," Mittford explained.

"Tell me more, my good friend… Tell me more!" Butler was all ears.

Mittford spent the next two hours recounting his findings and what had transpired in the bowels of The Johns Hopkins Hospital. How Albie Greenlaw met his end. How Velma Smith died in her sister's home. How there were several other suspicious deaths by electricity, going back to at least 1905. How the earlier deaths seemed to be concentrated in the upper echelons of society.

"Waldo, may I ask what has become of your bodyguard, Mr. Mulcahy?" Mittford asked after his hours-long discourse.

"I had to terminate his employment. His tactics had become too heavy-handed for my liking. He had a way of threatening people that was quite disquieting…"

It was Mittford's turn to interrupt. "Yes, I was on the receiving side of his intimidation tactics. He visited my office before I left for Baltimore and New Jersey and threatened to inflict bodily harm if I continued pursuing the investigation into your son's death."

"Precisely my point, good sir. Precisely my point. His service to my company was invaluable for a time, but quickly outlived its usefulness," said Butler. "I later found out from a contact in Baltimore, highly placed in City Hall, that Mulcahy had been defrocked as a police officer there for exceeding his authority and for physically abusing suspects in his custody. There was even a rumor that he had killed a suspect in an interrogation room.'

Mittford blanched at Butler's description of just how far Mulcahy would have gone to protect his former boss. It was not a pleasant thought that the threats would have been carried out. It was even more unnerving to realize that Mulcahy would have acted independently of his boss's wishes. A pensive silence replaced the conversation.

"With Mulcahy out of the picture, is staying in New Jersey the best decision?" Mittford wondered. *"I was happy here in Allentown, until that beast threatened me within an inch of my life."*

After what seemed like an eternity, Mittford spoke once more.

"Waldo, I am convinced that it is best for me to take the Essex Club up on its generous offer. I am not getting any younger and being called out in the middle of the night to deliver a baby no longer gives me the pride it once did. I am imagining that the worst thing I will have to deal with at the Essex is something one of its members doesn't want to take home to his wife, if you know what I mean…"

"Yes, of course. I wholeheartedly agree that you have to make the choice that is best for you, Doctor Mittford. I wish you well in your future endeavors," Butler said, indicating that their conversation and meeting was at an end.

Both men stood and extended their hands to each other. They exchanged a firm handshake and Doctor Robert Mittford bid goodbye to his former patient.

Mittford returned to his now-silent office and unlocked the door, Dust and cobwebs were everywhere; had he been staying, it would have taken weeks to return the rooms to a standard of cleanliness expected of a medical practice. That would be up to the new occupant, a young and newly licensed physician coming from The Johns Hopkins Hospital and the tutelage of his friend, Dr. Henry Mills Hurd. Mittford knew that it would be a good while before

Allentown's captains of industry and their families would trust such a young and experienced doctor, but that was no longer his concern.

Working from the back rooms of the practice out towards the door, Mittford was careful to collect anything of either sentimental or research value, especially his personal notes not directly related to patient care. He would leave behind all patient medical notes in hopes that the new doctor would use them to establish his credibility.

Mittford also left behind a selection of instruments, mostly obstetric tools, that could prove useful in the new doctor's future. They were expensive even in Mittford's early days as a doctor and were certainly more expensive now; he felt he was doing the right thing by leaving them behind as a gift to the arriving physician. *"Besides, I think I have delivered my last baby and done my last female exam,"* he chuckled to himself.

Reaching the door and having stacked three crates of papers and equipment just outside, Mittford turned back and took one last wistful look over his once-vibrant practice. He had been in Allentown since his earliest days as an independent physician and there were fond memories. Memories of hundreds of babies born. Memories of old people whose time on earth had come to an end. Memories of horrific factory accidents. Memories of the candid conversations he had had with certain individuals, Waldo Emerson Butler included, about their dalliances and the dangers they posed to their own and their wives' health. He was satisfied that he had done his best to keep his patients healthy and was leaving on his own terms.

Locking the door for one final time, Mittford nodded to the Negro porter he had hired to transport his cargo to the train station, a mere three blocks away. He was on his way back to West Orange. The next train that would get him there was scheduled to depart in less than an hour. Including a stop in Philadelphia, the train trip would take about four hours.

Chapter Eighteen: Falling Into Place
1908-1909

Back in West Orange, Doctor Robert Mittford hired a horse-drawn hansom to take him from the train station to the Essex Country Club. He had left with not much more than an overnight bag and had returned with more medical equipment and supplies than he could carry. He would need help to get the crates to his corner suite at the country club.

It would take most of the next week for Mittford to unpack and arrange his suite. The former sitting room, which opened directly into the hallway, was to become his office and examination room. His sleeping quarters and private lavatory would be closed off during his consulting hours.

Outside the door, where there were several chairs lined up against the opposite wall to serve as a waiting room, Mittford had hung his shingle: "Robert Mittford, MD." It clearly marked his territory. Below it, he had hung a shingle, carved by a local craftsman, clearly stating his office hours: "Monday through Thursday, 9 a.m. to 2 p.m."

His benefactors, the Essex Country Club's Board of Directors, had agreed to his 4-day work week, with the proviso that Mittford could not close his door at the end of the day if there were still prospective patients waiting in the hallway. Some days, there were none – but there were days where Mittford did not get away from the patients until well after 5 p.m. It was not a terribly grueling schedule, but in order to continue receiving his free room-and-board plus a discretionary stipend, Mittford had to agree to those terms.

Some days, it was blistered feet and sore throats. Others, it was prescriptions for calomel, the standard mercury-based treatment for syphilis. His most memorable days were those spent educating younger men on the workings of the female body before their wedding night. Mittford's knowledge of the fairer sex was purely clinical; he had no practical experience of his own to draw from.

It wasn't that Mittford lacked interest in romance. Rather, it was purely a matter of available time. His studies and detective work allowed very little room for courtship and he felt it would be unfair to any lady for him to be more attentive to his work than to her needs.

During his non-working hours, Mittford was consumed by his investigation into the suspicious electrocutions. Rarely a day went by without his poring over copious notes and newspapers. It might be weeks between discoveries of more suspicious electrocutions, but each one got the same attention. Mittford did not discriminate based on race or social standing; the poorest of the poor in the most derelict of slums got the same level of interest as did the richest of the rich in the most stately homes.

Granted, it was less likely that the poorer class neighborhoods were being electrified to the same degree as the wealthy, but they were still the day laborers, the A-rabbers, and others who kept cities bustling with activity. It was when their paths crossed with the upper echelons that there was a greater likelihood of an electrical mishap.

Such was the case of Dmitri Vlassos, a Greek immigrant who had been hired in Baltimore by the Calverts of Ruxton Heights as their cook. Vlassos's obituary, like that of Velma Smith, appeared briefly in the Baltimore newspapers. It simply stated, *"Accidental Death: Dmitri Vlassos, recently arrived from Greece, died on Tuesday at the home of his employer, the Calvert family of Ruxton Heights. The City Coroner determined the cause of death to be accidental electrocution."* Mittford knew that he had to get to Baltimore to interview the other servants in the Calvert home and determine what exactly had happened.

He would leave immediately after office hours on Thursday and spend the weekend in Baltimore.

It was several days after Dmitri's accidental electrocution when the newspaper item appeared, but Mittford decided it would still be worth his time to visit the Calvert mansion. Once there, he would wheedle and cajole his way into an inspection of the area where Dmitri died in hopes of finding a faulty switch like the ones that Albie Greenlaw had demonstrated before his own gruesome demise.

*   *   *   *   *

The kitchen of the Calvert's Ruxton Heights mansion had just been electrified a week or so before Dmitri Vlassos reported for work. He spoke little English, but the Calverts already had a member of staff who could translate and assist Dmitri with developing his English abilities. It turned out that they would need to devote little effort to Dmitri's language skills.

It was Dmitri's second day on the job. He had been filling a metal pot with water to begin making a seafood stew. Setting the pot down on a metal table next to the stove, but still keeping a hand on the u-shaped handle, Dmitri reached for the switch that operated the fan above the stove. There was a momentary flash of light, followed by a blood-curdling scream. As the electrical current arced from the switch, through Dmitri's upper body, and to ground through the pot and table, his muscles convulsed violently. Within seconds, his torso and arms were in their final, fatal spasms.

The stench of burning human flesh wafted quickly through the kitchen, nauseating the rest of the workers. Fortunately, the fuse for the fan circuit blew before Dmitri's lifeless body was cooked to a crisp. The electricity now off, his body fell to the floor, but smoke continued wafting upwards from his thick head of black hair. Dmitri was dead; everybody knew there was no way he could have survived.

The Calvert family's purser finally telephoned the City Coroner, who in turn contacted the Baltimore Police Department. It took them over an hour to arrive at the mansion, time in which the stench from Dmitri's burned corpse wafted further throughout the home. Even Mrs. Calvert was sickened by the smell – and she was in her dressing room on the second floor.

The coroner and the duty officer from the Northern District were perfunctory in their assessment. They interviewed the purser and the rest of the kitchen staff, determining that Dmitri had died accidentally. There would be no inquest, no safety inspection, nothing official that could provide deeper detail on the exact cause of the electrical fault that had killed Dmitri Vlassos. It would be up to Mittford to do the deep detective work and uncover something, anything, that was inconsistent with the findings of the coroner and the detectives.

*   *   *   *   *

Before departing West Orange, Mittford sent a telegram to Sparky, who was still residing at George Ruth's saloon:

ENROUTE BALTIMORE STOP SUSPICIOUS CIRCUMSTANCES OF DEATH NEED YOUR IMMED ATTENTION STOP MEET ME NINE AM SATURDAY YOUR LOCATION STOP MITTFORD

Sparky had just returned to the saloon when the Western Union boy delivered the telegram. Puzzled at first, Sparky knew that Mittford would only reach out if there was something genuinely amiss. Seamus and Willie were usually given weekends off, but the gravity of Mittford's telegram suggested that Sparky's two employees should be present when Mittford arrived.

"Seamus, I need you to be here tomorrow morning at nine. Doctor Mittford is coming in by train and needs to speak with us about an urgent matter," Sparky explained. "Could you telephone Willie, through Mrs. Marshall, and make arrangements for him to be here as well?"

"Of course, Sparky. Will you be tellin' us what has ol' Doc Mittford so stirred up?" Seamus replied.

Passing the yellow Western Union print to Seamus, Sparky said, "Read the telegram for yourself. It doesn't tell us very much. He doesn't even say which death is suspicious. For all I know, he could be talking about Miss Velma Smith, may she rest in peace."

On the train, Doctor Mittford could not rid himself of the notion that he had overlooked something. The conversation between the two men at the diner haunted his dreams and made him wonder if Sparky was directly involved. Before overhearing that conversation, there was no reason to even suspect Sparky. The situation had changed after hearing how Garfield was allegedly sending purloined components to Sparky at a rate considerably less expensive than purchasing from a supplier like a hardware store.

Was it possible that Sparky was simply being duped by John Garfield? Mittford could not be sure with the limited information he had assembled in West Orange. Garfield was perhaps the least interesting person in town. His life lacked variety and it did not appear that Garfield engaged with other human beings on a regular basis.

Mittford arrived in Baltimore and headed for the upscale Hotel Belvedere. His stipend from the Essex Country Club was more than adequate to cover his expenses for an occasional weekend away. He reached the hotel around 10 p.m. and was escorted to his room by a bellboy obviously groveling for a tip. Mittford handed the boy, still smooth-skinned and capable of singing soprano in the choir, two quarters and nonchalantly waved the interloper away. "Thank you, Doctor Mittford. I hope you enjoy your stay," the boy squeaked all too cheerily.

In less an hour after his arrival, Mittford was fast asleep. That sleep turned fitful an hour into the night, during what would eventually become known as "rapid eye movement sleep.". John Garfield's face haunted him. In the dreams, that face would morph from that of a meek janitor to that of a maniacal demon. Each time, Mittford woke in a cold sweat. He had to solve the causes of the suspicious deaths –

and soon. Not knowing was more stress than any practical exam he had endured in medical school.

Fully awake before dawn and well before the high society hotel would even consider serving breakfast, Mittford took the time to write down notes about his dreams. The vision of Garfield as a demon would not go away, nor would the subliminal image of a hooded Garfield slinking around in the shadows of the General Electric complex rummaging through piles of discarded electrical components.

After about an hour lost in his thoughts and notes, Mittford decided that he needed coffee. Room service was available at the Belvedere, but not before 7 a.m., so he would have to convince the night clerk and kitchen staff to share their own coffee with him. It was an easy undertaking as the night clerk had been instructed to take care of guests' needs regardless of the hour.

When the kitchen boy delivered the coffee to Mittford's table in the corner of the lobby, the doctor noticed that the boy likely was of Mediterranean descent, possibly even Greek. Mittford had studied Greek in college and decided to greet the boy in what he hoped would be his native language.

"Good Morning! Can you help me?" Mittford inquired in Greek. The boy smiled at Mittford's near-perfect pronunciation.

"Sir, I speak perfect English. I was born in America and have gone to American schools. My parents still speak nothing but Greek at home, though," the boy explained.

"Young man, do you know of a Dmitri Vlassos?" Mittford asked.

"Yes, sir. He was our neighbor and died horribly," the boy said as he crossed himself. "I think he worked for the Calvert family north of town."

"Can you tell me more? I am curious about the manner of his death. It is a hobby of mine," Mittford explained. "And... will you tell me your name?"

"Of course, sir. My name is Nicholas Niarchos. My friends all call me 'Nicky'."

"Nicky it is. So... tell me what you know of Mr. Vlassos's demise," Mittford said, raising one eyebrow quizzically.

"Mr. Vlassos didn't speak a lot of English. A few words, nothing more. He knew I worked in a hotel kitchen and was constantly asking me about what my work was like."

"I see..." Mittford acknowledged with a nod.

"Our kitchen here at the Belvedere had electricity even before I started working. Everyone is used to it and can't remember what it was like to be without it. Mr. Vlassos, on the other hand, lived in a house that was still lit by candles and gaslights," Nicky said.

"Interesting," Mittford responded. "Did you teach Mr. Vlassos anything about safety around electricity?"

"Yes, and he always paid attention when I talked to him about how dangerous electricity could be."

"So there is no way he would have gotten too close to water while his hand was on a switch?"

"No, sir. Mr. Vlassos knew better than that."

"Nicky, you've been a big help. Thank you so much for speaking with me."

Mittford was now convinced that it was Garfield's faulty components to blame for the electrocutions. Nicky's description of Vlassos's attentiveness and understanding of the dangers of electricity offset any chance that the ground fault was merely an accident. The hands on the clock could not move fast enough for Mittford; he knew he would be at Ruth's Saloon long before the appointed hour and hoped that Mrs. Ruth would have a hearty breakfast laid out for the lodgers. He would gladly pay for a home-cooked meal as he was growing weary of the *haute cuisine* served at both the Essex Country Club and the Hotel Belvedere.

Chapter Nineteen: Astonished
Baltimore, 1909

In Ruth's Saloon, the smell of bacon and burned toast hung in the air. The remains of the morning meal still on their plates, Mittford, Sparky, and Seamus discussed what Mittford had discovered in his investigation. Mittford noticed that Willie Washington was conspicuously absent but started his explanation anyway. He described how the overheard conversation in the West Orange diner had the scales teetering and the most recent death in Baltimore tipped the scales towards foul play.

"Doctor Mittford, are you saying that my friend, John Garfield, is behind the deaths?" Sparky asked incredulously.

"I am saying exactly that, Mr. Thompson," Mittford replied, his voice deadpan.

Turning to Seamus, Sparky asked, "Where is Willie this morning?"

"Boss, I have no idea where our friend is this morning. He has always been as punctual as the Camden Station clock." Seamus appeared nervous that his fellow apprentice had not yet appeared in the saloon doorway.

"Let's listen to what the good doctor has to say. Then we'll go to Division Street and find out what has happened to Willie," Sparky said reassuringly. "Can you telephone Mrs. Marshall once more and see if there is any news of Freddie?" Seamus went back to the Ruth's telephone and did as his boss instructed.

Mittford continued explaining his theory of foul play and how John Garfield was his prime suspect. He also alluded to the possibility that Sparky could be complicit in the deaths, or even the two apprentices. Mittford calmly said that if any of them knew of Garfield's activity and how he stole the components, it would certainly convince a jury to render a guilty verdict in court, no matter what the charges might have been,

Sparky spoke first. "Doctor Mittford, I was a good friend to John Garfield in his times of need. He was demoted by Mr. Edison for pulling pranks on the engineers. I aided him in those pranks, but only to make them happen. I never knew the 'why' of what he was asking me to do.

"Please tell me more, Sparky," said Mittford.

"The one that sticks in my mind is when he polished the terrazzo floor with vegetable oil and lard. It was as slippery as ice. I didn't know what he had done, but he asked me to call the engineers to one of the laboratories, which I did."

"Go on," Mittford urged in acknowledgment.

"The first engineer, a personal friend of Mr. Edison, scurried up the hallway. When he hit the polished area, his feet went out from under him and he fell, breaking his arm. The next engineer, seeing his colleague writhing in pain, quickened his step to aid his friend. He, too, fell – but on top of the injured man. Aside from the moans of pain, the only thing we could hear was John Garfield belly-laughing so loudly it echoed down the corridor. I knew right then and there that I could no longer participate in the pranks and would have to fess up when the time came."

"So that was the end of your employment by Mr. Edison?"

"I was left with no choice but to offer my resignation. When I did, I also put in writing that the mastermind prankster was John Garfield, not me," Sparky explained, his face somber.

Interrupting the conversation and quite out of breath, Seamus blurted out, "Boss... Doctor Mittford... it seems that Willie is missing. He was supposed to meet us here for breakfast and Mrs. Marshall told me that she gave Mrs. Washington the message. Willie did not come home last night."

A few minutes later, the newsboy dropped off the morning paper on the bar. The headline was disturbing: "POLICE INVESTIGATE ELECTROCUTION" and it was subtitled "Foul Play Suspected." Sparky and Mittford looked at each other; they both immediately drew the same conclusion that Freddie was a suspect, even without reading the article. It was all just too coincidental. Regardless, Mittford read aloud:

"Before sunset yesterday evening, a cousin visiting from out of town was electrocuted at the Calvert mansion in Ruxton Heights north of the city. The young man, whose name is not given here to respect the family's wish for privacy, was pronounced dead at the scene. This is the second electrocution to take place at the Calvert mansion in recent weeks. Foul play is suspected, as a Negro, one Freddie Washington of Division Street, was seen leaving the home shortly before the gruesome accident. Police from

the Northern District arrested Washington at a nearby streetcar stop. It appears that Washington was involved in wiring the mansion for electricity."

Sparky's face turned white as a sheet. "That's two accidents at the Calvert place in less than a year. First it was one of their cooks, and now a cousin from out of town. Seamus, Freddie, and I wired the place to Mr. Calvert's specifications. Freddie is one of the most trustworthy men I know, and he would never have intentionally mis-wired a switch or outlet." Sparky's nervous pace was rapid-fire. He knew that he, too, could be implicated in the accidental deaths – now that he also knew of John Garfield's nefarious procurement of defective components from the General Electric trash heap.

Mittford remained calm, despite Sparky's stridence. "Sparky, we have to get to the Northern District lock-up and seek Freddie's release. I might not be in Baltimore's inner circle, but I do know a lawyer or two in town."

Sparky spoke up, "Doc, I hope you can help us get Freddie off the hook. I know what Baltimore police are capable of – and Freddie's skin color makes it that much worse. He's guilty until proven innocent and we can't let that stand."

For his part, Seamus knew exactly what could happen if electrical parts were defective or not connected properly. He had experience in that area from his work at the Harland-Wolff shipyard in Ireland. On more than one occasion, he had stopped a drunken foreman from reversing the connections on switches in the First Class passenger compartments on the "*SS Corinthic*". It was the same foreman that had cost Seamus his job and forced their immigration to America. He shuddered at the memory. Not only had it cost him his job, but his marriage as well: a letter from Bridgit just a week earlier told Seamus that she was going back to Ireland and that he should not follow her.

Returning to the present with a shudder, Seamus finally joined the conversation. "I trust Freddie with my life. He knows as much as I do about electricity and wiring – and he is honest almost to a fault. I agree with Sparky that Freddie could not be responsible for the accident at the Calvert place."

* * * * *

The previous afternoon, Freddie had, on his own volition, gone back to the Calvert mansion. His intent was to check on the servants and how they were adapting to the electrified modern conveniences. It was purely circumstantial that the visiting relative's mishap took place while he was there. He wasn't even in the part of the mansion where visitors were accommodated.

While Freddie was in the kitchen having a snack provided by the Calvert's cook, the lights suddenly dimmed and returned to their normal brightness. Within seconds, a woman's screams could be heard all the way to the kitchen. The sound was perhaps amplified by the dumbwaiter shaft used to deliver food to the dining room and private quarters of the mansion.

Freddie knew there was something amiss with the electricity, based on his experience and the dimming lights. He wanted to go to the upper floor of the mansion to investigate, but the cook told him that it would not be a good idea to venture up there – especially once the signal bells started ringing. The cook explained that "when them bells start a-ringing like that, all hell's broken loose and a Negro man up there in working man's clothes would just not be right. No, sir!"

Freddie nodded in agreement, thanked the cook for the delicious snack, and headed to the Ruxton streetcar stop to return home. Walking towards the streetcar stop, Freddie was passed by a police wagon on its way to the mansion. He thought nothing of it until, about a half an hour later, the police wagon returned, and four uniformed white officers alighted, quickly encircling Freddie Washington.

"Don't try anything funny, boy!" one of the officers ordered. "Cooperate and you won't get hurt." The smirk on the officer's face and the derisive tone in his voice suggested something else was in store for Freddie Washington.

Freddie, as he had been taught by his mother, went into deferential mode and responded with a contrite "Yes, sir."

Before Freddie could say anything further, he was hit across the backs of his legs with one of the officers' nightsticks. He dropped immediately to his knees in excruciating pain. Freddie was afraid for his life, and rightfully so.

Over the next several minutes, the officers summarily beat Freddie, all the while accusing him of intentionally manipulating the switch in the Calvert mansion bedroom, the one that caused the death of the visiting cousin. The officers were experienced enough to know how to deliver a beat-down without leaving significant marks or breaking bones. Still, Freddie's lip was split and his eyes blackened from the beating. It was in this condition that he was taken to the Northern District station house and thrown in a filthy holding cell, accused of murder.

It was in that cell, with only a bucket for a toilet, that Freddie Washington spent the night. Rats roamed freely throughout the dank cell, and it took all of Freddie's energy to keep them at bay. Throughout the night, the lights in his cell would be turned on and off at erratic intervals ranging anywhere from five to thirty minutes. Each time the lights came on, one of the jailers would rap on the bars of the cell with his nightstick. The lights and the noise kept Freddie in a state of constant disorientation. By morning, he was in a mental state where he would have confessed to anything just to make the sensory torture stop.

*   *   *   *   *

Sparky, Mittford, and Seamus reached the Northern District station around noon. At first, they were stonewalled by the Desk Sergeant. It was Mittford's strident insistence that one of his patients, Freddie Washington, might be in need of medical attention that eventually got them access to Freddie in his cell.

Escorted to the holding cells by an overweight and under-bathed jailer, only Doctor Mittford was allowed into

217

the cell with Freddie. As Mittford passed the jailer in the cell's doorway, the jailer mumbled "Nigger lover..." under his breath. Mitford turned and glared at the man. "Stop right there, sir... *Mister* Washington is my patient and I will treat him the same as I would any other human being, with compassion and respect. I demand that you treat me with the respect a Doctor of Medicine deserves." The tone in Mittford's voice was icy. The jailer shrugged his shoulders, turned around, and walked away without another sound.

Mittford thoroughly examined Freddie. Everywhere he palpated, Freddie winced in pain. The beating had been thorough. No bones were broken, thankfully, and there did not appear to be any internal organ damage.

"Freddie, when you last passed water, did you notice any blood?" Mittford asked.

"No, sir. There was no blood, but it was lots darker than what I normally see," Freddie replied.

"That means you are dehydrated and need to drink lots of water," Mittford explained.

"Guard!" Mittford bellowed, "my patient has been deprived of food and water long enough. I insist that you bring him as much clean water as he cares to drink – and not any of that revolting stuff you use to wash out the cells. I will not be treating this man for dysentery caused by your malfeasance." The jailer understood that Mittford meant business and was not a man to trifle with.

An hour or so later, David Bellamy, Esquire, arrived at the Northern District station. Bellamy had been called by Mittford as they left Ruth's Saloon. Bellamy and Mittford had a long friendship going back to their college days and it was only when they chose their own professional paths that they lost contact. Still, because both men were Freemasons, the bond of kinship was strong and Mittford knew he could count on his old friend to help Freddie Washington get released from the trumped-up charges. The Baltimore City State's Attorney was also a Freemason – another connection that could be worked in Freddie's favor.

By suppertime, everything had fallen into place. Bellamy convinced the City State's Attorney that the evidence against Freddie Washington was circumstantial and that it was simply a case of "wrong place, wrong time," compounded by Freddie's skin color and the mistrust the City Police Department.

By 6 p.m., Freddie was once again a free man. He was still in severe pain from the beating, so Doctor Mittford went with Freddie to his Division Street home and administered a sedative once Charity had bathed her husband and tucked him into bed. Freddie slept for almost all of the next two days. When Sparky checked on his apprentice the next day, he told Charity that Freddie didn't have to worry about work for the next two weeks, and that he would receive his full pay.

After Freddie had been taken care of, Sparky asked David Bellamy if he should have any legal concerns based on what Doctor Mittford had discovered in New Jersey.

"Were you knowingly installing defective parts?" Bellamy asked.

"Of course not. I had no reason not to trust my old friend, John Garfield. I did not know that he was padding his pockets by including defective parts... Edison's trash... in my orders," Sparky explained.

"Would you testify to that under oath?" Bellamy queried.

"I certainly would," Sparky asserted.

"Then I do not think you have any exposure in this matter. It was Mister Garfield's responsibility entirely – assuming that Doctor Mittford's theory can be proven," Bellamy intoned.

"I think we need to go to West Orange," said Mittford with a nod.

Sparky turned to his apprentice, "Seamus, would you go to Camden Station and reserve five Second-Class seats for us, please?"

Seamus returned about three-quarters of an hour later with tickets in hand for the 3 o'clock train. They would be in West Orange before midnight.

"Mrs. Ruth," Sparky called out, "could you be so kind as to prepare a picnic basket for us to take on the train? There is no dining car on our train, and we will surely be hungry by the time we get to our destination. I can think of nothing better than your fine cooking, ma'am."

As they were getting ready to leave Ruth's Saloon, Mikey stopped them short. "Mr. Sparky," he began with a tremble in his voice, "I don't want to go to New Jersey. I want to go back home to my parents and the farm. I don't like all this traveling and living in rooming houses. It just ain't for me."

"What are you saying, Mikey?" Sparky asked with a furrowed brow.

"I'm saying that it's time for us to go our separate ways," Mikey replied. "I don't like all this travel. When I am someplace new, I can't sleep until I am sure I'm safe… and that took several days in here in Baltimore."

"I understand," Sparky replied. "We are from different worlds, I think. I grew up with the noise of a neighborhood. You, on the other hand, came from the quietness of a farm."

Seamus was conspicuously quiet as Mikey offered his resignation. He knew that Mikey was at times a liability to their team. *"After all,"* Seamus thought, *"the poor lad couldn't keep two boxes of switches straight."*

Chapter Twenty: Back in New Jersey
Late 1909

Fortunately for Sparky Thompson and his team, they were between contracts when Doctor Mittford suggested the trip to New Jersey. The four men, Mittford, Sparky, Seamus, and Bellamy, boarded a train at nearby Camden Station heading for West Orange. They would have to change trains in Philadelphia and again in Newark before reaching their destination.

Mittford telephoned ahead and arranged accommodation for the other three men in the semi-opulence of the Essex Club. It was from there that they would continue their investigation into the circumstances surrounding the suspicious electrocutions. None of the men were trained detectives; regardless, they were as a group able to analyze the nuances of each of the electrocutions that Mittford had catalogued over the past three years.

Edgar Allan Butler. Henrietta Frankel. Velma Smith. The Calvert cousin. The Lawyers Hill incidents. All of them had happened since John Garfield had been demoted by Thomas Edison. Mittford was sure there were others, perhaps in cities or towns from which Mittford did not receive newspapers.

Seamus silently squirmed in his seat every time Henrietta Frankel's name came up on the victim list. He knew what he had done to the switch in Henrietta's bedroom. What Seamus didn't know was that Henrietta had been electrocuted by another switch, the one in the hallway outside her bedroom. That switch had come from the defective stock supplied by John Garfield. Only the Harrisburg police report mentioned the specific switch that was believed to have been responsible for Henrietta's untimely death, and it was not the one that Seamus had tampered with.

*　*　*　*　*

Detective Sean Mulcahy, newly-hired by the West Orange Police Department, had turned over a new leaf. Not long after Doctor Mittford left Allentown, Waldo Emerson Butler terminated Mulcahy's employment. Butler told Mulcahy unequivocally that the termination was because of the heavy-handedness of Mulcahy's interactions with other people, and Doctor Mittford in particular.

Butler, too, had had a change of heart in the months following his son's death. He was no longer a conniving wheeler-dealer; instead, he had become the city's leading philanthropist and donated nearly half of his business profits to Allentown charities. It was in the spirit of goodwill that Butler agreed to write a glowing letter of recommendation for Mulcahy. It was strong enough that it overrode the smudge put on Mulcahy's career by his dismissal from the Baltimore City Police Department.

On the West Orange police force less than a year, Mulcahy was already the model detective and was not going to do anything to jeopardize the second chance he had been given. He followed approved investigative procedures and no longer resorted to physical abuse as a means of interrogation. His conviction rate was nearly flawless, and the prosecutors repeatedly praised his diligence and thoroughness.

Mulcahy's latest case involved a badly decomposed body found in a wooded area just inside the city limits. The body showed signs of trauma to the head and it was only discernible from the tattered clothing and undergarments that the body was that of an adult female. The shape of the compressed skull intrigued Sean Mulcahy. It was too regular to have been accidentally inflicted; the fracture seemed to be almost a perfect circle. Mulcahy had seen similar wounds before, while walking his beat in Baltimore.

"I tell you," Mulcahy began, "when I was in Baltimore, I saw plenty of this sort of thing, mostly in the slums around the factories and shipyards. It was usually a ball peen hammer…"

The other police officers and detectives looked at Mulcahy; their expressions highlighted their interest in what he had to say. Most of them had never even seen a dead body, much less had to examine one for signs of foul play. Yet, here was Detective Sean Mulcahy showing them how the powers of observation coupled with experience could provide insight on the cause of death. Even the West Orange Coroner was intrigued.

"Our first step is to go canvass the areas around the factories and workshops. Door-to-door if necessary. Ask the housewives if any of their lady friends have suddenly disappeared. We need to identify this poor soul before we can start looking for suspects," Mulcahy explained, his tone almost like a college professor in front of a room full of first-year students. "I am willing to bet that the victim will be the wife of a factory worker, perhaps one in his cups and prone to violence. Some men just can't handle strong drink and the slightest infraction by their wife or children will send them into a rage."

It took the West Orange Police less than a week to solve the case under Mulcahy's leadership. It was indeed the wife of a factory worker; both had recently arrived from Scandinavia and were down on their luck. The factory worker barely made enough money to pay the rent and put food on the table – but the wife constantly overspent.

"Enough is enough!" he bellowed after spending several hours in a bar drinking on a Friday evening. Grabbing his wife by the arm, he dragged her to the ravine at the edge of town, swearing at her in Swedish the entire time. He had a hammer hidden in one of the deep pockets of his factory overalls.

"You brought me to this godforsaken place," she hissed. "I would go back to Sweden, to Mama and Papa, in a minute if there were enough money for my passage."

His rage peaked. "You'll... do... nothing... of the... kind!"

She spun around to get away from him; her rebellious action sent him completely over the edge. Reaching into his pocket, he grabbed the hammer and swung it with the full force of his now-muscled right arm. The ball end of the hammer struck her occipital bone, fracturing it and driving bone fragments into her brain stem. She was instantly paralyzed and rendered speechless by the wound – but was fully conscious as he mercilessly beat and kicked her to death, which thankfully came quickly.

Using only his hands and the hammer as a scraping tool, the man covered his dead wife's body with woodland detritus and topsoil. The makeshift grave was deep enough that any odor of decomposition would have been masked, but not enough that the semi-skeletal remains would not eventually be uncovered by the elements. It was those remains that were uncovered, in the third stage of decomposition, less than a month after the murder.

Once arrested, the man confessed to his wife's demise. He was quickly processed and tried for his crime. Though the prosecutor asked for the maximum penalty then allowed by New Jersey law – the electric chair – the presiding judge took a compassionate view, "Because Mr. Swalgaard confessed to his crime, I am inclined towards leniency. His sentence is life in prison without the possibility of parole."

Mulcahy had scored another victory and again proven his skills as an investigator. Little did he know that those skills would soon be put to the test again. The next case, however, would be considerably more complex and involve one of West Orange's captains of industry, Thomas Alva Edison.

*   *   *   *   *

After a restful night in the superior accommodations of the Essex Club, Mittford, Sparky, Seamus, and Bellamy assembled for breakfast in the main dining room. The fare there was considerably more epicurean than what was served at Ruth's Saloon. On a sideboard were all types of breads and pastries, a steam table with an assortment of meats and other delectables, and a never-ending supply of coffee. Eggs or omelets were cooked-to-order on request. The enticing smells increased their hunger, as they contents of Mrs. Ruth's picnic basket had been devoured quite early the previous evening.

"Gentlemen," Bellamy began, "I believe our first order of business is to visit the local constabulary and present our case to their detectives."

Doctor Mittford agreed. "It would be in our best interest to start there and not confront the Edison establishment directly. It is my opinion that such an approach will result in a wall of silence."

Sparky, on the other hand, suggested a completely different approach. "Perhaps I should re-establish contact with John Garfield and see if I can get information out of him that we could turn over to the police..." Sparky surprised even himself with the willingness to exploit his past relationship with Garfield.

Mittford quickly agreed that Sparky's plan had the most merit and the greatest likelihood of producing immediate and tangible results. Sparky and Garfield were once friends, despite the fact that Sparky's letter to Edison had resulted in John Garfield's punitive demotion. "It certainly is worth a try," Mittford said with a nod.

"I know where Mr. Garfield lives," Mittford offered. "I can take you all there and we can wait outside, across the street on the benches, while Sparky engages Garfield in a reconciliatory conversation."

Bellamy, who initially was quite circumspect about Sparky's idea, finally agreed. "The conversation between Sparky and Mr. Garfield would be admissible in court as it would be a direct recollection of that exchange, and not a third-party observation. Remember, gentlemen, our goal is to get a conviction and to completely clear Freddie Washington's name."

Sparky was concerned that he would be nervous in any discussion with John Garfield. Once friends, they were only connected by the business of Garfield supplying electrical parts to Sparky at a reduced cost. Would Garfield take Sparky's entreaty as an effort to rekindle their friendship? If Garfield assumed that to be true, it would make eliciting information from him that much easier.

Mittford provided his personal observations about the whistles and schedule for the General Electric plant. He told Sparky that Garfield would return home for lunch within minutes of the mid-day whistle and that there would be roughly an hour before the "return to work" whistle sounded. "That," Mittford asserted, "should be enough time for you to make your presence known and to set up a meeting later in the day after Garfield is done with his work for the day. Perhaps you could convince him to join you for pie and coffee at the diner down the street? Garfield knows none of us and we would be there in case of trouble."

Sparky thought for a moment before responding. "Yes, Doctor Mittford, I do believe that a relaxed atmosphere would be best for us to have our discussion. It has been nearly five years since I spoke to John Garfield in person, so anything between us will be tense at first."

Finishing their sumptuous breakfast, the men got up to leave. It was nearly eleven a.m. and they had just over an hour to get to 272 ½ Snyder Street. Bellamy suggested they hail a hansom cab or ask that the Essex Club provide one from their livery stable. Mittford telephoned the Essex Club concierge and was granted access to a horse and buggy as long as he would need it. The equine-powered transportation was much more reliable than any of the motorcars the Essex club had to offer.

The men reached Snyder Street just as the mid-day whistle sounded. "It will be about ten minutes before Garfield rides up on his bicycle," Mittford commented.

"I will be ready," Sparky replied. "What bench gives me the best place to see John approaching?"

"I always sat in the one directly across the street when I was observing Garfield's movements," said Mittford.

Sparky set off across the street while Mittford drove the buggy a few hundred feet away and turned it around. They would be in a good position from which to observe the initial encounter between Sparky and John Garfield, but not so close as to draw Garfield's attention and suspicion. Everything seemed to be falling into place.

As Mittford had predicted, John Garfield rode up on his bicycle a little more than ten minutes after the mid-day whistle. Seeing Garfield approach, Sparky got up from his bench and crossed the street, stopping at the base of the stairs for 272 Snyder Street. It was there that he called out to his former friend.

"John? John Garfield? Do you remember me? Sparky Thompson... we used to work together at the Edison factory," Sparky beamed. "It's been what? Five years, maybe?"

"Sparky, you old codger. Yes, it has been about five years since I was punished by Mr. Edison, no thanks to you." The acrimony and contempt in Garfield's voice was clear. He still held Sparky responsible for the fate of his career.

"John, it's time we buried the hatchet and let bygones be bygones," Sparky pleaded. "How about we meet at the corner diner for pie and coffee after you've had your supper?"

"I guess we could share some time together to catch up, but that doesn't mean we will be friends again," John said, his voice devoid of any emotion.

"We'll see where things go... See you around 7? It will be my treat," said Sparky.

"As it should be," Garfield observed as he gave a short nod. "See you then."

John Garfield turned and climbed the stairs to his meager apartment. He had little in the way of provisions. Some smoked ham, some day-old bread and a pot of mustard would have to suffice for his supper. Making a sandwich, he ate in silence as he usually did; however, his mind was far from silent.

"Out of the blue, that bastard shows up on my doorstep and expects everything to be back the way they were? Who is he trying to fool? I don't trust Sparky Thompson any more than I trust the devil himself," Garfield mused silently. *"Still, I should at least make an effort to appear cordial."*

Chapter Twenty-One: The Game is Afoot
West Orange, New Jersey

John Garfield left his apartment a few minutes before seven p.m. It was a five-minute walk to the diner, and he wanted to be on time for his meeting with Sparky. For his part, Sparky was already there, along with his trio of covert observers. Mittford, Seamus, and Bellamy had taken a booth a few feet away from Sparky and were talking quietly among themselves as Garfield entered.

"John! Over here. Come have a seat!" Sparky called out jovially. "They have apple and raspberry pie tonight, and the coffee is fresh and hot."

Garfield scanned the diner. He wanted to be sure that there were no other General Electric men nearby. The last thing he needed was for one of them to recognize Sparky and assume they were conspiring. Garfield had, for the past five years, managed to conceal his thefts of defective switches and outlets. Sparky, too, was unaware of his escapades – or so John Garfield wrongly assumed.

"How have you been, John?" Sparky asked as his former friend sat down.

"Still sweeping floors and cleaning up after the hoity-toity engineers, no thanks to you," Garfield replied. It was quite obvious that he still held Sparky in contempt and responsible for his current plight.

"Maybe we can get over that rough patch and become friends again?" Sparky cajoled.

"I told you last night when you proposed this meeting that I was not sure we would ever go back to the way we were," John Garfield countered.

"Let's not focus on that for now. We've got a few years to catch up on," said Sparky, trying to get the conversation back to a more friendly tone.

For a few minutes, the two men sat quietly, sipping on their piping-hot coffee. Garfield preferred his with milk and several spoonsful of sugar, while Sparky took his black. Sparky chuckled as he remembered the sticky mess that was left behind when Garfield had spilled the last few ounces of a cup on the workshop floor. It was an honest accident and not one of the pranks that resulted in John Garfield's punitive demotion a few years later.

Garfield, on the other hand, seethed with anger. He could not remember anything positive about their relationship, even though Sparky was complicit in the long string of pranks. *"This bastard owes me something,"* Garfield thought to himself as their pie was served.

The waitress finally out of earshot, John Garfield became quite talkative.

"Sparky, how have those switches and outlets been working out for you? You know… the ones that I have been sending you at cut-rate prices…" Garfield asked.

"Well… it certainly is less expensive to get them from you than it is from the local hardware merchant. There is the mark-up and all," Sparky replied.

"Of course…" John Garfield agreed, taking a huge bite of apple pie and a swig from his cup. Again, there was a silent pause before Garfield spoke again, "this pie certainly is the best in town, I have to say."

Garfield had already decided that he would spill the beans to Sparky and divulge that he had sent defective parts in most of the shipments. He was simply waiting for the proper time to give Sparky that information. Garfield wanted the revelation to have maximum effect and to deflate his former friend's ego.

Before Garfield could put his own plan into motion, Sparky leaned in conspiratorially and said in a very soft voice, "John Garfield, I know that you have been mixing defective parts in with your shipments."

Garfield glared at Sparky. "Prove it."

"How else could you afford to sell the parts so cheaply?" Sparky countered.

"Mr. Edison might have demoted me, but he didn't take away my access to..." Garfield stopped short, suddenly realizing that Sparky was spinning a trap, one that he did not plan to fall into.

"John, can you live with yourself, knowing that several people have died because of your greed?" Sparky asked.

"Died? Preposterous! There is no way people could have been killed unless the parts were mis-wired or something." Garfield was quickly becoming argumentative, having been backed into a corner. His fight-or-flight response was on high alert.

Seamus Conaty, still seated several booths away, heard Garfield's words. Nervous perspiration beaded up on his chest and in the small of his back. He knew that Garfield was correct: mis-wiring certainly could be the cause of an accidental electrocution, as the case of Henrietta Frankel had proven. He had, after all, intentionally mis-wired the switch in her boudoir in hopes that it would put an end to her advances; he never intended for her to be killed. If Sparky ever found out, Seamus knew that he would be turned over to the authorities.

Sparky responded to Garfield's allegation. "Not so fast, John... It doesn't take an engineer to figure out that tampering with the contacts inside a switch and the terminals in an outlet could cause fatal results. You know that as well as I do. Need I elaborate on the names of the dead?"

Garfield's eyes started darting around the room, sensing that he had been overheard. First, David Bellamy stood up; Garfield noticed the movement with some trepidation, a concerned look on his face.

Before Bellamy could take a single step, a large and imposing gentlemen two booths away and nearest the door stood up. It was Detective Sean Mulcahy. He had overheard every word of the conversation between the two men.

"John Garfield, you are under arrest. I need you to come along quietly. We want to ask you some questions at the station house," Mulcahy said, his voice sounding very official. Quietly and without further ado, Mulcahy put Garfield in handcuffs and marched him outside to a horse-drawn paddy wagon that had just pulled up. As Garfield stepped up into the wagon, he stepped right in the middle of a still-warm pile of horse droppings; a good amount of defecatory matter stuck to his shoe and carried the odor with him to the police station.

As the paddy wagon drove away, Sparky was confused. How did the police know to be at the diner at that particular time? It didn't add up. Doc Mittford and David Bellamy were both adamant that it was premature to contact the police without having concrete evidence.

David Bellamy spoke first. "Sparky, Doc Mittford, Seamus... I know the Chief of Police here in West Orange and I took the liberty of informing him that he might be able to arrest a murderer right in his own town. He was all ears as I told him the story. I could not divulge to you that I had done this, as Sparky's plan would not have worked out as well as it did. I apologize for the subterfuge, but it only made sense to do it this way."

Seamus was only slightly calmed by this revelation. He had immediately recognized Mulcahy from his previous encounters in Baltimore and Allentown. Mulcahy, on the other hand, had no memory of ever encountering Seamus, so the fear was misplaced. The West Orange Police Department had their man on multiple charges: theft of property and murder – the latter of which was at the time a capital offense in the State of New Jersey.

Chapter Twenty-Two: John Garfield
In His Own Words, 1910

Taken from a written statement to the West Orange Police Department:

I had been with Mr. Edison since he moved the company from Menlo Park to West Orange all the way back in 1887. That's over twenty years. I think, besides Mr. Edison himself, that's one of the longest times for any current employee.

What do I have to show for it? A sore back, blistered hands, and tired feet. Sure, I was never a shining star of an employee – but you would think after all those years, I would get some recognition, a decent increase in my wages, and perhaps a promotion.

I started off as an apprentice to one of the electrical fabricators and had, after fifteen years, worked up to assembling components by myself. Switches, outlets, fuse boxes. All of them. It was one stupid prank that stopped my apprenticeship in its tracks and relegated me to janitor, all because I let my friend, Sparky, take the blame without confessing to my own involvement. Instead, my involvement was made known after Sparky was dismissed, and I now regret that I had remained silent.

We all thought it was funny when we replaced wax in the janitor's floor cleaning equipment with lard. They looked the same on the gray terrazzo floors, but the lard was as slippery as new ice on a pond in winter. After two of Edison's favored engineers slipped and fell, one of them breaking his arm, Sparky decided it would be best to fess up. I chose to stay silent, hoping that there would be no repercussions.

As Sparky was being escorted off the site, he handed Mr. Edison an envelope. In that envelope was a letter describing how the prank had been set up and how I was the mastermind. It was me who replaced the wax with the lard, All Sparky did was summon the engineers to his workbench in a manner that would bring them across the slick floor. We did not expect their falls to be as severe as they were.

A few hours after Sparky left, Mr. Edison himself summoned me to the inner offices that he occupied. He gave me a thorough and vitriolic dressing-down, then demoted me and told me that I would never work anywhere else within a hundred miles of General Electric. "I'll see to that," Edison snarled at me when he rendered the demotion. I knew he was serious and accepted what he had in store for me. It was either that or head south to work in the jungles of Panama and help dig that canal. From what I had read in the newspapers, laborers there were paid decent wages – but were always at risk to pestilence and disease.

After a few penitent months, I reached out to Sparky at the address he gave me. He was in Allentown, I think. I told him that I could provide him with components well below the price he could get them by ordering through the local hardware store. What I didn't tell him was that I had easy access to the spoils of General Electric. The components that did not pass inspection, the ones that were defective right from the start. It was because of my access as the janitor that I was able to claim these discarded items as my very own. They would have ended up in the trash anyway. I couldn't see the point of wasting them.

With Sparky's needs being met, I finagled a deal with one of the boys in the shipping department to pack an occasional defective item into every few orders. With this arrangement, the reject would replace a tested and approved component in the shipment, making it a totally random process. There was no way of tracing the defect back to its origin as hardware stores and electricians placed orders that were filled weeks later and then sat in their own stocks for weeks, if not months, after delivery. It was my little bit of revenge against Mr. Edison and General Electric: their good name would be dirtied and their reliability questioned – even though they manufactured and provided the greatest share of electric parts for installation in homes and businesses.

Electricity was supposed to be a safer alternative to gaslights and candles. There was little risk of fire from electricity – unless a user did something stupid like replacing a fuse with a copper penny. I made sure that what I was doing would cast doubt on its safety and hopefully damage Mr. Edison's reputation in some meaningful way. It would be his retribution for treating me so badly...

"Mr. Garfield," Detective Sean Mulcahy interrupted, "you have a Constitutional guarantee against self-incrimination. If you continue with this voluntary statement, your words may be used against you in a court of law. Do you wish to continue?" Mulcahy knew that Garfield was running right up to the line where he would admit that he intended for people to get hurt by the defective switches and outlets. He also recognized that Garfield's behavior was focused on himself, with no acknowledgment of the difference between right and wrong. *"The man has no conscience,"* Mulcahy thought to himself as the interview was coming to a close.

"I already told you everything, Detective. In writing, no less. Edison and General Electric deserve what comes to them. I would like to speak to my lawyer now, please," said Garfield.

John Garfield did not have enough money to pay for a lawyer. It was fortunate for him that Essex County had a pool of lawyers who would take on *pro bono* work, especially in capital cases. Attorneys were assigned by rotation, week by week. If no cases came up during an attorney's assigned week, the rotation passed to the next attorney.

Ralph Blanchard, Esquire, was ultimately assigned to defend John Garfield. During their initial discussions of the case, Blanchard was very direct and told Garfield that he would use every trick in the book to get the case dismissed or achieve a "not guilty" verdict. It was Blanchard's standard legal *patois* when he was taking on a new case.

Blanchard didn't personally care whether the suspect was innocent or guilty. Each case meant another chance to get his name into the papers and for the case to be sensationalized, which the newspapers of the day did with gusto, but usually not until the trial had actually started. He never shared his personal lust for attention with his clients, instead leading them to believe that he was their best hope for salvation and exoneration. Still, John Garfield remained skeptical of his chances for acquittal as he knew that Doctor Mittford had been thorough and had presented a compelling case to the West Orange authorities.

Blanchard used every legal trick in the book, starting with a motion for a change of venue. He asserted in a written brief to Judge Steven Benoit that an impartial jury was unlikely because of the heavy influence Thomas Edison and General Electric had on the people of West Orange. Judge Benoit denied the motion almost immediately, telling Blanchard in unequivocal terms that such a motion was inappropriate until the jury selection process. "It is there, during the interviews of prospective jurors, that you can determine their affiliation with Mr. Edison or General Electric – or even if such an affiliation exists," Benoit explained in his response.

Chapter Twenty-Three: Trial
Newark, Summer, 1910

"All rise!" the bailiff bellowed. Everyone in the filled-to-capacity courtroom stood up in unison. The noise was a loud reminder of the respect given to a courtroom, the presiding judge, and the law.

"Hear Ye! Hear Ye! Hear Ye! The Superior Court of Essex County in the State of New Jersey is now in session, the Honorable Judge Steven Benoit presiding."

Judge Benoit climbed the steps of the dais and stood behind his bench for a moment, scanning the room, seeing that Thomas Alva Edison himself was in the gallery. Benoit did his best not to acknowledge anyone in particular in the gallery and especially not Edison. The last thing he wanted was to be accused of favoritism.

"Please be seated," Benoit said as he sat down in his own seat, adjusting his voluminous robe for comfort. Turning to his right, he made eye contact with the bailiff. "What matter comes before the court this day?" Benoit asked.

The bailiff replied, "Your Honor, it is the criminal matter of the State of New Jersey vs. John Garfield of 227 ½ Snyder Street, West Orange. Mr. Garfield is charged with multiple crimes, to include murder and theft of property belonging to the General Electric Company of West Orange."

"Will the counsel for the State and for the Defendant make their introductions?" the judge ordered.

"Thomas Willmer for the State, Your Honor."

"Ralph Blanchard for the defense, Your Honor."

"Gentlemen, you may proceed with opening statements," said Judge Benoit.

Willmer spoke first. "Gentlemen of the jury…" He spent the next thirty minutes elaborating on the scheme concocted by John Garfield. His main arguments would be that Garfield wanted revenge on Thomas Edison and the General Electric Company and that his depraved indifference to the resulting loss of human life was grounds for a guilty verdict on the charge of murder. Keeping the introductory remarks to an overview of the case, Willmer wanted to be sure that he had plenty of legal ammunition once he began calling witnesses. He was eloquent and convincing, his pitch and volume rising for effect – a technique that had served him well in his orations since law school. Willmer offered that "the defendant may not have meant to cause grievous bodily harm or even death, but his actions showed a blatant disregard for human life."

After a brief pause for effect, Willmer continued. "The defendant, Mr. John Garfield, simply did not care if his actions would or would not cause harm to the innocent victims and their families." Willmer continued by listing the names of the dead: "Edgar Allan Butler... Henrietta Frankel... Albert Greenlaw... the Negro woman, Velma Smith... Dmitri Vlassos, full of hope for the American dream... These are just the victims we know about. There have been – or certainly will be – others. His behavior, presumably for vengeance against his employer, recklessly endangered human life."

Being a prosecutor suited Thomas Willmer, Esquire. Life as a defense attorney would have compromised his principles: his Puritanical outlook and conscience would not allow him to defend someone who had committed heinous crimes. Defense attorneys relied on technicalities in the law to secure acquittals and he firmly believed that the law was the law and that criminals needed to be punished.

Ralph Blanchard, on the other hand, was at times unscrupulous and at other times a blustering buffoon. His courtroom theatrics were as legendary as his disregard for the rule of law. It was his job as defense counsel to help his clients walk out of court as free men (or women, in only a handful of cases), "The law be damned," he was fond of saying.

Blanchard and Willmer were well-matched as legal adversaries and had met in court numerous times before. Neither man had a statistical advantage over the other in jury trials: their individual success rates were almost even.

Blanchard's opening remarks were as long and as eloquent as Willmer's. Instead of focusing on the law, however, Blanchard took a tack that emphasized the circumstantial nature of the evidence that the prosecution would present. "The prosecution," he asserted, "cannot prove without casting a shadow of doubt that my client was responsible for the deaths of at least four individuals. With that doubt, and a possible death sentence hanging over my client's head, you must vote unanimously to acquit."

Willmer rose quickly and spoke up over his opponent, "Objection, Your Honor... counsel is attempting to influence the jury by jumping ahead to the penalty phase and his client has not yet been found guilty."

"Sustained. The jury will disregard the defense's commentary about the death penalty," Judge Benoit commanded. A chuckle rose from the gallery as Willmer had just embarrassed his opponent. It was the first time that the bloviating Blanchard had ever encountered an objection to his opening arguments; he knew he was in for a fight.

The wind now completely taken out of his sails, Blanchard managed to gracefully end his opening statement and avoid further embarrassment. He still had to defend his client to the best of his ability. Preparing for each day's session would be exhausting.

"Mr. Willmer, are you ready to call your first witness?"

"I am, Your Honor," Willmer replied. "The state calls Mr. Waldo Emerson Butler to the stand."

Butler had come all the way from Allentown to testify. Being questioned by the prosecution for over an hour, Butler described how he had lost his son to an electrical accident. He even talked of how the life insurance payout helped his company survive some hard times. Butler's testimony was emotional and compelling, but there was no so-called smoking gun that incriminated Garfield; there also was nothing exculpatory in his testimony, either.

"Your witness," Willmer said, turning Butler over to cross-examination by Ralph Blanchard.

"Mr. Butler, I am sorry for the loss of your son. That must have been hard on you and your wife," Blanchard began, trying to elicit an emotional response from the witness. "How much was the insurance pay-out after your son's demise?"

"One hundred thousand dollars," Butler replied. "I had taken out a double-indemnity policy several years earlier."

A collective gasp went up from the gallery; most of the observers were wage earners, not salaried businessmen That amount of money was more than 250 times what a skilled worker would make in a year and more than 50 times greater than what an administrative professional like an accountant would earn.

"Order... Order in the court!" Judge Benoit commanded as he rapped his solid walnut gavel on a matching sound block. The courtroom slowly settled back to silence.

"Mr. Butler, can you explain to the court what a double-indemnity policy is?" Blanchard asked. Butler spent the next several minutes explaining how, in the event of accidental death, a life insurance policy would pay double the declared value. He took great care to emphasize that the double-indemnity clause would only come into effect if the cause of death was *proven* to be accidental.

"What did the insurance company require as proof of accidental death?" Blanchard asked.

"A statement from a medical doctor or the jurisdiction's coroner," Butler answered.

Blanchard theatrically turned towards the jury as he posed the next question. "I see… was it the coroner who determined the cause of death to be accidental?"

"Yes… it was the Allentown coroner," was Butler's response.

Blanchard probed deeper. "Mr. Butler, is it possible that you paid someone to tamper with the electricity of your home to cause your son's death?" It was Blanchard's first overt attempt at creating reasonable doubt in the minds of the jury. If he could push a suggestion that transferred suspicion from his client to someone else, it increased the probability of a hung jury unable to render a unanimous verdict.

"Objection, Your Honor!" Willmer was on his feet before Butler had a chance to open his mouth to respond to Willmer's accusation. "Mr. Butler is not on trial."

"Overruled," replied the judge. "Mr. Blanchard, you may continue."

Once again facing the jury to gauge their reactions, Blanchard pressed the issue. "I ask you again, Mr. Butler, did you pay someone to tamper with the electricity in your home in hopes of causing harm to anyone in your family, perhaps someone covered by a generous life insurance policy?"

Butler glared at Blanchard as he spoke. "The only person I paid to do anything with the electricity supply to my home and my businesses was Sparky... Mr. Archibald Thompson. He is the most reliable and conscientious workman I have encountered. He would not... he could not... have done anything to intentionally cause harm to my family."

In the gallery, Doctor Robert Mittford squirmed in his seat, controlling the urge to speak. His investigation had discovered the defective switch in Edgar Allan Butler's room, and that would have shored up the prosecution's case; however, such a revelation would directly contradict the coroner's finding. It was too early in the case for the contradiction to be brought forward and Thomas Willmer had cautioned Blanchard to be circumspect in his upcoming testimony.

Suddenly, a puzzled look came over Robert Blanchard's face. He had realized that there were witnesses in the courtroom who probably should not be exposed to the testimony of the earlier witnesses, especially as the prosecution made its case.

"Your Honor, may I approach the bench?" Blanchard asked.

"Approach," Judge Benoit instructed. Willmer stood and approached the bench along with his opponent.

"Your Honor, it has been an oversight on my part and perhaps on the part of my opponent to allow upcoming witnesses to remain in your courtroom during the ongoing proceedings. I respectfully request that individuals on both the prosecution and defense witness lists be removed from the courtroom and sequestered until such time as they are called to the stand."

The judge turned to Thomas Willmer. "Mr. Willmer, what say you?"

"Your Honor, in this case, I agree with my opponent. Hearing earlier testimony could cloud the validity of later statements. This is a complicated case and we need each witness's testimony to stand on its own merits without influence from other witnesses."

Judge Benoit waved the two attorneys away from the dais. He had the witness lists in front of him. After briefly scanning the list, he looked up and addressed the room. "In my court, I want every trial to be fair and above reproach. Anything that could be prejudicial to either side's arguments needs to be scrutinized. It is in the interest of fairness that I am directing that the following individuals leave the courtroom at once and not return until they are summoned by the bailiff to appear." Judge Benoit then proceeded to read the list of both sides' witnesses without assigning the name to either the prosecution or the defense. Thomas Alva Edison and Dr. Robert Mittford were both on that list, as were Sparky Thomson, Sean Mulcahy, and Seamus Conaty. The list read, Benoit declared, "this court stands in recess until 2 p.m." and banged his gavel.

The trial continued for the entire week. At the end of the week, it was not clear which side had the advantage. The prosecution seemed to have proven its case, emphasizing the depraved indifference of John Garfield, through the testimony of Thomas Alva Edison and Archibald "Sparky" Thompson.

Sean Mulcahy was also on the prosecution's witness list. His testimony was compelling and seemed to confirm Garfield's guilt. Under cross-examination, however, Mulcahy's true self came out when he was pressed on his service as a Baltimore City police officer and as a bodyguard for Mr. Waldo Emerson Butler.

Seamus Conaty was the last prosecution witness to testify and he was decidedly nervous on the witness stand. Before beginning cross-examination, Blanchard stated for the record, "Your Honor, certain facts regarding Mr. Conaty's life in Ireland will come up during my cross-examination. I hope that the court and the jury will take Mr. Conaty's previous situation into account with regard to his credibility."

"Proceed," replied Judge Benoit.

Somehow, Blanchard had managed to find out about Seamus's escapades at the Harland-Wolff shipyard in

Ireland. He used that situation to completely destroy Seamus's credibility. Thomas Willmer recognized it as a blow to the prosecution's case; they had to *prove* the guilt of the defendant, while the defense only had to inject the premise of reasonable doubt.

"Mr. Conaty, is it true that an altercation at the shipyard was the reason for your emigration to the United States?" Blanchard probed.

"Objection, Your Honor!" Willmer roared. "Mr. Conaty is not on trial here."

Blanchard responded, "The question speaks to the credibility of this witness, Your Honor."

"I will allow it. Mr. Blanchard, you may continue."

It took nearly an hour before Blanchard was able to elicit the puzzle-piece response from Seamus Conaty and determine his culpability in the Harland-Wolff incident. Blanchard also brought to the fore the idea that Seamus was skilled beyond the apprentice level and had been nearing his journeyman qualification – something that completely puzzled Sparky Thompson. *"Why had Seamus presented himself as a lowly laborer?"* Sparky thought to himself. *"I thought he was just a quick learner..."* What never came out in Seamus's testimony was his observation of the defective switch in Edgar Allan Butler's bedroom.

Blanchard's list of witnesses for the defense was miniscule compared to the prosecution's. There were only three defense witnesses: John Garfield himself, another janitor from the General Electric factory, and Seamus Conaty's wife, Bridgit, who had been preparing for her return to Ireland from Butler's Allentown mansion. Blachard managed to delay her departure after interviewing Butler's domestic staff. He sensed the tension between Bridgit and Seamus and thought that he could exploit that to the benefit of his client.

"Mrs. Conaty, I thank you for delaying your return to Ireland so that you could testify before this court," Blanchard began. "Will you share with us the tone of your present relationship with your husband, Seamus Conaty?"

Bridgit still retained certain Irish affectations in her speech. "Aye, sir. Me husband turned out to be an evil man, prone to the influences of other women. He paid me no attention at all after he left domestic service and stopped sending money after a while…"

This seemed to be the opening Blanchard needed to discredit nearly all of Seamus's testimony. Thankfully,

Bridgit had remained unaware of Seamus's intentions for the demise of Henrietta Frankel. Had she been aware, Blanchard could have exploited that as well. Instead, he relied on the coroner's report which clearly stated which switch had caused Henrietta's death. Seamus breathed a sigh of relief when he realized that it wasn't the switch he had sabotaged. He relaxed even more when his estranged wife's testimony was finished. She had not mentioned the Baltimore incident and it appeared that Blanchard was completely unaware of it as well.

On Friday morning, both the prosecution and defense presented their closing arguments. Both emphasized the complexity of the case. Blanchard's defense focused on how the prosecution had not established a firm connection between Garfield and the suspicious deaths. Prosecutor Willmer, on the other hand, hammered the concept of Garfield's blatant disregard for human life and how his actions were clear evidence of that, with supporting testimony from Thomas Alva Edison and Archibald "Sparky" Thompson.

Closing arguments complete, Judge Benoit gave the jury his instructions. "Gentlemen of the jury, you have one task before you: to decide the guilt or innocence of Mr. John

Garfield, who has been charged with murder. You must only examine the evidence before you. Nothing more, nothing less. And... because in the State of New Jersey, a conviction on a charge of murder carries with it the possibility of a death sentence, your verdict must be unanimous."

Judge Benoit turned to the bailiff. "Bailiff, escort the jury from the courtroom and see that their needs are met. They are not to have any contact with the outside until they have rendered a verdict." Benoit banged his gavel one final time, "This court stands in recess pending a verdict from the jury."

"All rise!" the bailiff ordered. Once the judge had returned to his chambers, the courtroom was abuzz with soft conversation in the gallery. The somber jurors filed past the spectators and reporters without making any comments. They understood the gravity of the situation before them.

A section of the Continental Hotel was used by the courthouse to billet jurors during deliberations. Once a trial was scheduled, the city would commandeer the rooms for the duration of the trial, thus ensuring that accommodations would be quickly available if the trial were to end and the jury sequestered for deliberations. Most of the hotel had the double beds, but not the county-reserved floor. Each of the eight rooms there were furnished with two single beds so that two jurors could be housed in a single room. It was not an ideal situation and tempers sometimes flared, but it got the job done.

Two of the eight rooms were reserved for the four bailiffs or police officers that would be assigned around the clock. Their purpose was to prevent jurors from having any contact with the outside, especially the press or family members, while deliberations were in progress.

Chapter Twenty-Four: Verdict
Summer, 1910

The jury deliberated through the weekend. On Sunday, a Catholic priest and a Protestant minister were both brought in on Sunday to conduct services for the faithful. The priest also heard confessions from the five Catholic men on the jury. Services complete, the twelve men were served a traditional Sunday dinner of roast beef, potatoes, vegetables and copious amounts of coffee or tea. Alcohol, except for Communion wine brought by the men of the cloth, was prohibited as its presence could be detrimental to the decorum and gravity of the situation.

Around 5 p.m., the jury foreman, Alfred Stapleton, called for a vote. They were still deadlocked at ten votes guilty and two votes not guilty. Unfortunately, it was never the same ten men voting to convict. If it had been the same alignment after several votes, Stapleton could have informed Judge Benoit of their deadlock and offered the possibility of a hung jury. He knew that, because of the malleability of the alignment, they would eventually get to a unanimous verdict as it was always a different point in the trial that was leading to the votes swinging back and forth.

Stapleton, one of the Catholics, had been elected foreman because of his impressive education. He was a psychologist who had studied under the eminent Dr. William James at Harvard and was currently a tenured faculty member at Seton Hall University in nearby South Orange. Stapleton looked professorial in his longish hair, VanDyke beard and *pince-nez* spectacles.

The remaining eleven men of the jury represented a cross-section of West Orange and were all dressed in their Sunday best. Laborers, shopkeepers, skilled tradesmen, factory workers, engineers, and business magnates were all represented; however, none of the jury members were current or past employees of General Electric. They had been excused during *voir dire* as the likelihood of being loyal to their employer would overshadow their impartiality.

"Gentlemen," Stapleton said somberly, "once again, we are ten to two in favor of conviction. Yet each time we have cast our ballots, it is two different men who have voted to acquit. I recommend that we each spend the remainder of this night in quiet discussion and prayerful meditation, considering once again how justice will be served in this case. We will reconvene tomorrow morning at 9 a.m."

"Bailiff!" Stapleton shouted, "The men are ready to be escorted to their overnight accommodations."

The jury quietly assembled and departed the courthouse for the short walk to a hotel across the square. There, they had been billeted two to a room since Friday. On Sundays, the hotel generally provided clean linens on each of the beds, so Stapleton suggested that there be some reallocation of room assignments after Sunday services; he silently hoped that such a reapportionment would cause a shift in votes. There was also a risk that the two recent "not guilty" voters would end up in the same room and become entrenched in their positions. Stapleton accepted that risk and pressed for the reshuffling of roommates.

At 8:30 on Monday morning, Stapleton called again for the bailiff to escort the jury back to the courthouse jury room. As promised, he called for a vote precisely at 9 a.m. "Gentlemen, once again we are faced with a vote of guilt or innocence. Instead of proceeding as we have with past ballots, I would like this round to be completely secret with no name attribution affixed to your vote. Can we agree that such an approach will relieve the pressure some of you perceive is being put on you to vote one way or the other."

Stapleton continued, "At the writing desk in the corner, each of you will record your vote and place it in the cherrywood box. After the rest of you have voted, I will cast my own and then tally the votes." He paused for effect. "Does anyone have any more questions or items they would like to discuss before we begin voting?"

A heavy silence hung over the room. Each man knew the gravity of the situation and what a "guilty" verdict could mean for John Garfield. Though the judge had some flexibility in sentencing, the charge of murder in New Jersey generally carried with it a sentence of death. The fact that New Jersey had in 1906 switched from hanging to electrocution as its means of execution was not lost on the jurors.

One by one, the men went to the writing desk and cast their votes. Each did as they were instructed, being careful not to divulge which direction they had cast their ballot. A few of the men spent several minutes agonizing over their votes; Stapleton recognized this and asked them to be quick with their decision.

It took over an hour for the eleven jurors to vote. Stapleton, as foreman, always voted last – but did not have to worry about casting a tie-breaking vote. Seeing that the other eleven were finished, Stapleton strode to the voting desk, convinced that they would reach a verdict after this round.

Professor Stapleton put the pen to paper and wrote his vote. "Guilty." The prosecution had convinced him of John Garfield's culpability in the deaths. The defense, on the other hand, had focused simply on discrediting the prosecution's witnesses.

"Gentlemen, everyone has voted, hopefully for the last time. Please bear with me as I count the votes,"

One by one, Stapleton tallied the votes, starting with his own. After that, the first five were all "guilty." The next four, too, were "guilty." The last two, which coincidentally seemed to be the contentious votes in each round, remained in the box. Stapleton's hand trembled as he unfolded each piece of paper. The first: "guilty." He could hardly breathe as he unfolded the twelfth and final ballot. s "Guilty." They had a unanimous verdict!

Pausing for a moment to catch his breath, Stapleton addressed the jurors. "Gentlemen, we are finally unanimous on the charge of murder. I would like us to take a moment for silent prayer and reflection before we call the bailiff in to have him tell the judge we have a verdict."

The room suddenly was so quiet that the only sound to be heard was the ticking of several pocket watches. Tick-tock. Tick-tock. It was unnerving to some of the men as they pondered the gravity of their decision.

"Bailiff?" Stapleton called. "Please inform Judge Benoit that we have reached a unanimous verdict."

About half an hour later, the twelve filed into the jury box and saw that the gallery was packed with spectators and reporters. They took their seats awaiting Judge Benoit's entry from his chambers. The low din of hushed conversations rose from the courtroom but was silenced as the door to the judge's chambers opened.

"All rise!" the bailiff commanded. "The Superior Court of Essex County in the State of New Jersey is once again in session, the Honorable Judge Steven Benoit presiding."

"Everyone, please take your seats," the judge instructed.

Addressing the jury, the judge looked Professor Stapleton in the eye as he spoke. "Gentlemen of the jury, have you reached a verdict?"

"We have, Your Honor." Stapleton passed a verdict sheet to the bailiff, who in turn handed it to the judge. Benoit was careful not to let any facial expressions give away what the verdict might be.

"Will the defendant and counsel please rise?" Benoit's request was really an order. John Garfield, Ralph Blanchard, and Thomas Willmer all stood in unison.

"Mister Foreman, what say you?" Benoit inquired.

"Your Honor, in the matter of the State of New Jersey vs. John Garfield, on the charge of murder through reckless endangerment and depraved indifference, the jury finds the defendant..." A hush fell over the courtroom. "Guilty as charged." Garfield's knees buckled as he leaned on Ralph Blanchard for support.

As the din rose to a roar, the judge once again banged his gavel to restore order. "Any further outbursts and I will clear this courtroom," said Benoit. His tone let the gallery know that he meant business.

"Gentlemen of the jury, the State of New Jersey thanks you for your service. You are discharged." There was a pregnant pause as the jurors filed out of the courtroom.

Addressing the defendant and counsel, Judge Benoit made a pronouncement. "John Garfield, you have been found guilty of murder by a jury of your peers. You are to be taken immediately into custody to await sentencing, which will take place at noon tomorrow in this courtroom." Benoit wanted to have plenty of time to consider his sentencing options. "This court is in recess until noon tomorrow." With a single rap from his gavel, Benoit stood and returned to his chambers. He knew he was in for a sleepless night. It was not his first capital case, but the decision he faced was still unsettling. Unmarried, Benoit was used to spending the night in his chambers; he preferred the quiet ambiance and paneled walls to his small studio apartment on the other side of town.

*   *   *   *   *

After retiring to his chambers, Benoit pored over case law and sentencing precedents. The Garfield case was unusual in that there was both motive and opportunity for the defendant to commit the crimes. Benoit believed the motive was revenge and the opportunity was presented in the access that Garfield had to the spoils of General Electric's processes. He also believed that it was Garfield's intent to cause harm to someone, just not necessarily a specific individual.

Around two a.m. on Tuesday morning, Judge Steven Benoit woke in a cold sweat. He knew what had to be done. He would be sentencing a man to death that very day.

Around seven a.m., Benoit grabbed his shaving kit and overnight bag before heading across the street to the gentlemen's club for calisthenics, breakfast, a barber's shave, a hot shower, and fresh clothes. He wanted to be completely presentable in the courtroom when he pronounced his sentence.

By nine, Benoit was back in his chambers and preparing his sentencing statement. It would, by necessity, be succinct. He would declare the terms of the sentence and the facility to which John Garfield was to be remanded.

At eleven-thirty, John Garfield was ushered from his cell and allowed to change into a suit for the sentencing. Once properly attired, Garfield was shackled and handcuffed; the chains rattled loudly as he walked the short distance from the holding cell to the hall outside the courtroom. A few minutes later, he was met by Ralph Blanchard outside the courtroom.

"Good morning, Mr. Blanchard," Garfield sneered. "Let's get on with it." Garfield had a premonition during the night that a death sentence was likely and it showed in his defiant attitude.

"Mr. Garfield, there is always a chance that Judge Benoit will be lenient," said Blanchard. "He is always thorough in his review of precedents for sentencing." Garfield recognized immediately that Blanchard was merely providing reassuring platitudes.

Entering the courtroom, Garfield noticed that the jury box was empty and that the gallery was full of reporters instead of just spectators. *The jury won't have to see the result of their verdict. How convenient...*" he thought sarcastically to himself. Thomas Willmer was seated at the prosecutor's table and there were armed police officers stationed at the door and all four corners of the room. Garfield noted their presence but did not necessarily understand their importance.

Precisely at noon, the door to Judge Benoit's chambers opened. "All rise!" the bailiff commanded. "The Superior Court in Essex County for the State of New Jersey is now in session, the Honorable Judge Steven Benoit presiding."

Once again, Judge Benoit instructed those present to take their seats. He spent a little more than a minute shuffling through the papers on his elevated desk. It was a delaying tactic that he used to collect his thoughts before rendering weighty decisions such as the one before him.

Benoit cleared his throat before speaking. "The defendant will please rise.' Garfield and Blanchard stood as one; Willmer also stood as a formality; his part in the proceedings was done and he was merely a spectator with a reserved seat.

"John Garfield, you have been found guilty of murder by a jury of your peers... As judge, I do have some flexibility in cases such as this when I impose a sentence; however, I believe that you had the three essential elements necessary for such a conviction. You were motivated by revenge, revenge against none other than the respectable Thomas Alva Edison. You were presented with an opportunity, access to the spoils of the General Electric Company, and, by your own admission in the statement presented as evidence by the West Orange Police Department, the intent to cause grievous bodily harm to someone. It is this concept of depraved indifference to the welfare of others that I am compelled to render my sentence."

Benoit looked directly into John Garfield's eyes before continuing, "It is the sentence of this court that you be remanded to the State Penitentiary in Trenton, there to await execution for your crimes at midnight, sixty days hence. May God have mercy on your soul."

"Bailiffs, remove the prisoner," Benoit ordered. A single rap of his gavel ended the trial.

Garfield remained still and silent. He had already resigned himself to this eventuality. He did not struggle when the bailiffs took him by the arms to lead him out of the courtroom. He did not look back at his attorney. Back in the holding cell, he silently changed out of the suit and into his previously-worn prisoner's garb of striped pajamas. He would soon be on his way to Trenton.

Chapter Twenty-Five: Dead Man Walking
Trenton, New Jersey, Fall of 1910

The Trenton State Prison had been in operation since 1836. A maximum-security facility, it housed the state's only electric chair. Dark, dreary, and poorly ventilated, new inmates were immediately accosted by a miasma of human waste, sweat, and dampness.

John Garfield arrived at the facility without fanfare. He was processed for admission and suffered the indignation of being stripped naked for chemical delousing, having his head shaved, and a body cavity search for contraband. Frog-marched naked down a damp corridor, he was then issued prison uniforms, toiletries and bed linens and finally assigned a cell. Because he had been remanded under a sentence of death, he would not have a cellmate and would remain largely isolated from the other prisoners.

Garfield noticed immediately that his cell contained a Bible. There was also a cross on the wall. The cross was a gift from the prison chaplain, while Bibles had been placed throughout the prison by The Gideons. *"How odd..."* Garfield thought to himself. *"Here I am a condemned man, condemned for murder, no less... and the churchies want me to find God."* Garfield chuckled, recognizing that his time at the prison would be short unless the Governor intervened with a stay of execution.

Having no record of belligerence or violence, Garfield was allowed the prison's maximum exercise and outdoor time, up to three hours a day. Except for mealtimes, where death row inmates were fed separately from the general population, he would not be able to directly interact with other prisoners. Outside, he would always be accompanied by a guard and the sharpshooters in the watchtowers would be ready to open fire at the slightest provocation.

After about a week, Garfield's boredom got the better of him. He decided that he would begin reading the Bible. Without much thought, he opened the Good Book approximately to the middle. His eyes fell on Psalm 118:8: *"It is better to trust in the Lord than to put confidence in man."*

As he flipped pages randomly, he stopped at another passage, Ephesians 2:8-9: *"For by grace are ye saved through faith; and that not of yourselves: it is the gift of God,"*. The pace at which he flipped back and forth through the Bible increased as long-suppressed memories of his Roman Catholic upbringing and schooling began to surface. He did, however, try to put memories of the ruler-bearing nuns out of his mind entirely. By the end of his second week of incarceration, he was asking for daily visits by a Catholic chaplain. The prison warden honored Garfield's request. "After all, he is a condemned man," the warden agreed.

Father William O'Herlihy, of the Dominican Order, had recently been assigned to the prison by the Diocese of Trenton at his own request. He felt that he could do the most good as a teacher and confessor to the inmates rather than as a parish priest, a role that he felt stifled his calling to ministry. John Garfield was Father O'Herlihy's first death row inmate and would not be his last.

Before their first meeting, Father O'Herlihy was given a full briefing on the case, the crimes, and the sentence handed down by Judge Benoit. Armed with this information, O'Herlihy was able to engage in substantive discussions with Garfield almost immediately.

"Father, I am resigned to my fate but want to make things right with God before I meet him," Garfield said when they first met. "I was raised by Catholic parents but drifted away from the Church as I got older."

"My son, the first step towards Absolution is making Confession," Father O'Herlihy replied. "Do you still remember the Sacrament of Confession?"

"Yes, Father. I believe I do," Garfield responded in a barely audible voice.

O'Herlihy sat on the single bed in Garfield's cell. Taking his purple stole from a pocket in his frock coat, the priest kissed it, placed it around his neck, and made the Sign of the Cross. Garfield recognized that it was time for him to begin his confession.

Kneeling next to the bed, Garfield placed his hands in the priest's and bowed his head. He knew not to make eye contact with Father O'Herlihy during confession.

Before John Garfield managed to get the first word of the Sacrament of Confession out of his mouth, Father O'Herlihy stopped him, noticing that one of the guards was just outside the cell. "Guard, I am a man of God, an ordained priest, hearing a convicted man's confession. He deserves the same privacy here as he would get in a private audience with His Holiness, the Pope, in the Vatican. Please remove yourself from earshot of this cell."

The guard was not the least bit interested in Garfield's confession, but as a Catholic himself, he understood.

"Yes, Father. I will be on the other side of that door. I am a Catholic myself and understand the sanctity of the confessional," the guard replied as if he had just been rebuked by a nun in a Catholic school classroom.

"You may continue, my son," O'Herlihy said to Garfield. "In the name of the Father, Son, and Holy Spirit, Amen."

"Bless me, Father, for I have sinned. It has been at least twenty years since my last confession… I have committed a mortal sin… many mortal sins, actually. I have stolen from my employer and intended to use the stolen goods to do harm to others. It was not my intent, but people died as a result of my misdeeds. I kneel before you convicted of my crimes and condemned to death. I want to be right with God before I meet Him face to face."

"The Lord appreciates a contrite heart and that you have recognized your sins and are sorry for them. There is no penance I can give you, as you have been sentenced by man to die for your crimes. That is the ultimate penance, my son. I do suggest that you continue reading your Bible every day in hopes that you will find solace in its words."

"Yes, Father, I am truly sorry for my sins and accept the punishment I will be given."

"Then you shall enter the Kingdom of Heaven as a forgiven sinner, your sins washed away through the blood of our Lord and Savior, Jesus Christ..." Making the sign of the cross, O'Herlihy pronounced, "You are forgiven in the name of the Father, Son, and Holy Spirit. Amen." O'Herlihy stayed with Garfield for another half an hour and ended their private time with the Lord's Prayer.

"John, I will be back tomorrow as you requested. If you have any other sins you would like to confess, I will hear your confession – but since you have confessed to the most mortal of sins, I will offer you the Holy Eucharist if you so desire."

"Yes, Father. I wish to receive Communion every day between now and my... you know..."

"Yes, John... until that very day," the Father acknowledged. He knew their time together needed to end.

"Guard!" O'Herlihy yelled. "I am ready to take my leave of Mr. Garfield."

John was from that point forward a model prisoner. When he wasn't exercising, he spent every waking moment reading his Bible or talking to Father O'Herlihy.

"Father, what will it be like in Heaven?" John asked one day.

"No one really knows for sure, John. The Bible gives us some insight, though. The Revelation of St. John, Chapters Four and Twenty-One, are the most descriptive. St. John was given a preview of Heaven by the Lord while he was a prisoner in the penal colony of Patmos. You should read those chapters, John."

"I will, Father. Are there any other places in the Bible that talk about heaven and what it will be like? I know I could read the whole Good Book, but it would be better for me to use the little time I have left to go where you lead me."

Father O'Herlihy's knowledge of the Bible, Hebrew, and Greek were being put to the test. As a Franciscan, he was expected to be a teacher – but this was an entirely different situation than any he had previously experienced. His student was a man condemned to death, looking for insight on what was to happen to his very soul.

Instead of teaching in lectures, Father O'Herlihy decided that leading Garfield in discussions about the Bible would be the best approach. Any question Garfield wanted to ask, they would discuss. Garfield also invited his guards to participate. There was no prohibition on such discussions as even death row inmates were encouraged to practice their religion. However, the guards did have to be careful that their involvement with a condemned man and his priest did not compromise their judgment, engender their sympathy, or elicit an emotional response.

Each visit from Father O'Herlihy was different. Some days, they just sat silently in meditative prayer. Others, they had lively discussions of Bible passages and their meanings. It all helped pass the time and to keep John Garfield's mind occupied on something other than his looming appointment with "Old Smokey."

*   *   *   *   *

The day before John Garfield's scheduled execution, the warden paid him a visit.

"John, it's nearly time… What would you like for your last meal? Anything you want… it's yours." The warden's voice was compassionate. He was simply doing his job; his tone belied his support of the death penalty.

"Warden, I would like a plate full of freshly shucked oysters… roast canvasback duck… potatoes… carrots… apple pie with ice cream and hot black coffee for dessert.

As it was late October, both the oysters and the duck were in season. Canvasback ducks were readily available from Delaware Bay and Susquehanna River market hunters. Oysters literally covered the bottom of the Chesapeake Bay and were harvested with sailing schooners known as skipjacks. It would be relatively easy for the warden to grant John Garfield's request.

"Yes, John. I can provide all of those things for your final meal. If you would like, Father O'Herlihy can join you – but he will have to be seated outside of your cell," said the warden.

"I would like that very much," John Garfield replied.

"Before we bring you your last meal, there are a few other details we must attend to," the warden began to explain. "First, we must shave your head and your lower legs. This will make sure you don't suffer in your final moments. I'll spare you the gory details, but there are other things that we must do so that you can retain your dignity even in death."

The warden had decided long ago that the best way to provide the condemned man with this information was to read from a prepared script with no deviation. He carefully read the checklist without emotion or embellishment. The process took the better part of fifteen minutes.

"Warden, I thank you for your compassion," Garfield said in a voice that was barely audible. "I'd like to write my good-bye letters now. When I am done with that, can you please bring Father O'Herlihy back to administer the Last Rites?"

"Guard," the warden said softly but firmly, "please bring Mister Garfield a pen and paper. As much paper as he needs." Garfield noticed that the warden had used a dignified "Mister" when giving instructions to the guard.

A few moments later, the guard returned with a pen and a dozen sheets of plain white paper. Garfield composed three letters. His hand shook as he wrote.

The first was to Sparky. Garfield apologized for the damage that he had done to their friendship. He admitted to making Sparky an unwitting pawn that he had taken advantage of their relationship to turn a tidy profit from the sale of defective parts, which he counted at 497 pieces sold to electricians or suppliers in New Jersey, Pennsylvania, and Maryland.

The second letter, written in a more formal style, was to Thomas Alva Edison. Garfield wrote that he accepted his punitive demotion, but did not understand how, after so many years, Edison had not forgiven Garfield for his misdeeds. "As I sit in prison awaiting my own death, I have learned that forgiveness is God's way. His Son, Jesus Christ, said to Peter that he should forgive seventy times seven. By my accounting, your score is still zero against that four hundred and ninety. As my final penance, I tell you, Mr. Edison, that there are more defective parts out there waiting to kill someone. I have repented for my sins, and I hope your good name is destroyed when the truth is revealed."

The final letter, to Father O'Herlihy, was more emotional than either of the previous two. Garfield thanked the priest for his compassion and for his insight into the Kingdom of Heaven. He closed the letter with "Father, I am ready to meet my Maker and I will see you again on the other side of the Pearly Gates."

*   *   *   *   *

The clock on the wall ticked past midnight and the telephone connected directly to the Governor's Office remained silent. One minute turned into two... two into three... three into four... With no call from the Governor, the warden intoned, "John Garfield, you have been sentenced to die for your crimes. May God have mercy on your soul."

The warden nodded to the executioner that it was time. The executioner energized the transformers that would provide an initial charge of 2450 volts. That process would take just over a minute.

At five minutes past midnight, the warden nodded again to the executioner. Pulling the circuit breaker to complete the circuit, John Garfield's body convulsed as the charge passed from the top of his head to his feet. Lights throughout the penitentiary dimmed and the inmates knew what was happening.

Garfield's heart stopped almost instantly. Clinically, he was dead. Following protocol, the executioner disengaged the breaker twenty seconds after he had engaged it.

There was a mandatory fifteen-second pause before the same process was repeated. Though he was already deceased, Garfield's body convulsed once again as the electricity caused contracture of every major muscle in his body. Once the electricity was turned off, Garfield's body went limp. The process was complete, and the prison's physician pronounced John Garfield dead from cardiac arrest.

Chapter Twenty-Six: Completed Circuit
1911, After Garfield's Execution

Sitting on a hillock in Ilchester, on the Howard County side of the Patapsco River and upstream of the Bloede hydroelectric dam, Creighton Manor had just been wired for electricity. The dam, which began generating electricity in 1908 mainly for mills along the river, first supplied power to Ellicott City and Catonsville and the power transmission lines had finally reached Ilchester.

In the early days of electrification, it was normal for the new lights to dim whenever someone flipped a switch in another room on the same circuit. This time was different: the dimming of the lights was accompanied by a loud thud in the room immediately above wealthy industrialist J. Morris Creighton's expansive private library on the first floor.

Sitting in that library, Creighton thought nothing of the noise he had heard. Perhaps one of his two daughters had dropped something and would soon be calling for an appropriately humble and groveling servant to clean up a mess. He tilted his head, raised a single eyebrow, and harrumphed at being disturbed. Hearing no more noise, he returned to smoking his pipe as he read a recently acquired copy of Gustave Flaubert's *Madame Bovary*.

The library's shelves were filled floor to ceiling with leather-bound books, some of which were rare First Editions of works by authors like James Fenimore Cooper or Charles Dickens. Visitors to the Creighton home and the surrounding pastoral estate always wanted to spend time in the library, to smell the old leather, and to fawn over Creighton's collection. He, too, loved the smell of old leather – even if it was a little musty.

Creighton's eldest daughter, Cora Mae, had just retired upstairs for the evening. She and her younger sister, Emma Sue, had shared a three-room suite on the second floor since they were young girls. Two of the rooms were for sleeping and the third room was where the two marriageable daughters kept their expansive wardrobes and expensive cosmetics – most of which were imported from Paris.

Emma Sue was out on the town with her current beau, Thomas Herrington Slater. Thomas (no one *ever* called him 'Tom' or 'Tommy') was from a comparable family in the social and economic stratosphere of the county and lived several miles away. His family was one of the first to acquire a motorcar; Slater's father had gone all the way to Martinsburg, West Virginia, to purchase a Norwalk Touring Car straight from the factory.

With Emma Sue out for the evening, Cora Mae was left alone with her own books, novels that J. Morris Creighton would have called "trashy books for women, not worth the paper they are printed on. Too much emotion and pining for affection for grown men to waste their time on."

After his wife, Ruby, had died of unexplained causes while Emma Sue was still in diapers, J. Morris Creighton had raised the two girls on his own – with the assistance of a nanny, a governess, a cook, several maids, a driver, and a butler, that is. He had a self-imposed rule to spend no less than thirty minutes and not more than an hour with the girls each day, plus Sundays for church and a formal mid-day meal. Creighton was anything but a hands-on, loving father; he was the product of his own upbringing where male affection was rarely shown, the affectations of wealth were always on display, and all child-rearing responsibility fell squarely on the mother and her servants.

J. Morris Creighton was also obsessed with keeping everything in "tip-top working order," as he would say, so there was a constant stream of handymen and laborers scurrying about the Manor. He was, after all, a captain of industry and it would not be proper for his home to be in anything other than tip-top condition. He spared no expense to ensure that his dear Creighton Manor was always equipped with the latest in modern conveniences. That was how Creighton Manor came to be the first electrified home in that part of town. Creighton also owned an interest in the nearby Bloede hydroelectric plant.

Thomas Slater walked Emma Sue to the door after their night on the town. They had eaten dinner at one of the finest restaurants and had seen a traveling Sarah Bernhardt play at a Baltimore theatre. By the time Slater brought Emma home, it was just past midnight.

'Thomas, thank you for a wonderful evening," Emma cooed as they stood in the shadows on the massive front porch. As she took his hands in hers, her voice dropped nearly to a whisper. "You may kiss me if you wish," she said. It wasn't as though they had never kissed before; rather, that Thomas waited like a gentleman for her invitation.

Thomas leaned in. He could feel Emma Sue's warm breath on his neck. He could smell her perfume... expensive perfume from Paris, not the cheap stuff he had smelled on less fortunate women of the evening trying to hide their need for a bath. In the combined moonlight and soft light shining through the curtained windows of the library, Emma Sue's skin seemed to glow.

Their kiss was slow and gentle at first, but quickly grew in fervor and intensity. When she was alone with Thomas, Emma Sue was anything *but* a lady and would throw propriety to the wind. As long as they were out of sight from prying eyes, it was full steam ahead... up to a point. If Thomas's hands roamed to regions where they shouldn't, he would get a firm slap on the hand and the kissing would end right then and there – or at least until they were alone again.

*   *   *   *   *

Thomas often had conversations with his cronies at the local gentlemen's club about their conquests. It was normal locker room banter as the men showered and dressed for their workday. His friend, Frank Eager, had a secret crush on Emma Sue Creighton and was always curious about what he might be missing.

"Thomas, how did your evening with Emma Sue go?" Frank asked after their calisthenics one morning.

Thomas smiled and teased, "Why do you want to know, Frank? I think you might be trying to take my girl from me."

Frank wished for that more than anything else. It was the subject of many of his dreams and fantasies. There were times he could almost feel the warmth of Emma Sue's skin against his own; it was from those dreams that he usually awakened in the middle of the night.

As Frank turned away in frustration, Thomas said, "I will tell you, though, that Emma Sue Creighton is all flirt and no fuck."

*   *   *   *   *

Tonight was no different. Thomas eventually crossed the line, with his right hand grazing her left breast more firmly than it should have. The grope was titillating to Emma Sue, but she still grunted with righteous indignation and slapped his hand away "Good night, Mister Slater!" Emma made it clear that this was the end of their evening. Rolling her eyes as she smoothed out her crinoline dress, she turned and went into Creighton Manor. Once her back was turned, though, she was smiling broadly: Thomas Herrington Slater was wrapped around her finger and she knew it. As long as she kept her honor and deflected his advances, he would be like a puppy begging for a treat.

Inside the expansive entry foyer and its intricately carved wood panels and hand-hewn staircase, Emma Sue was met by the night maid, one of the lowest positions on the household staff. It was the poor woman's duty to see to the bedtime needs of the Creighton sisters when they came home from who-knows-where at all hours of the night. She had been sitting on a straight-backed bench in the foyer for several hours, relieved by one of the other maids only to take care of bodily functions.

"Miss Creighton, welcome back," said a weary Mary, the night maid.

"It is good to be home, Mary. Mr. Slater just walked me to the door a few moments ago," Emma Sue explained, a blush spreading across her cheeks.

Mary knew that it had been longer than a few moments. The 1911 Norwalk Touring Car's engine was far from quiet; in fact, it had awakened Mary from a momentary head-bobbing doze. She was wide awake when Emma Sue reached the front door almost thirty minutes later. Mary could only imagine what was happening on the other side of that door, but she had a pretty good idea.

"Shall I help you dress for bed, Miss Creighton?" Mary asked.

"Yes, Mary. This corset is killing me," Emma Sue intimated. Sharing simple statements of fact with the lower servants was never inappropriate. Besides, getting out of a steel-boned corset was a two-person job.

After peeking into the library to see that her father was fast asleep in his favorite chair and snoring quite loudly, Emma Sue ascended the staircase with Mary trailing dutifully behind. Reaching the shared dressing room, Emma Sue paused to let Mary enter the room first to turn on the new electric lights. As Mary fumbled in the dark for the switch, she tripped over something on the floor and stumbled forward into the room.

Emma Sue, somewhat miffed that her maid had taken such an unladylike and unceremonious fall, reached back into the upstairs hallway to turn on a light switch there. The hallway was quickly bathed in incandescent light which partially illuminated the entrance to the sisters' dressing room.

Emma Sue cocked her head trying to see who or what was lying immobile on the floor. Mary, well into the dressing room, turned to look behind her. Both women recognized almost simultaneously that the shape on the floor was Miss Cora Mae Creighton. Their screams brought a now wide-awake J. Morris Creighton and the entire household staff running to the second floor.

J. Morris Creighton recognized from his prostrate daughter's posture and lack of movement that she was probably dead. Kneeling by Cora Mae's side, he checked for a carotid pulse and found none. Turning to the head housekeeper, Mrs. MacDonald, he ordered, "Ring for the doctor… and the undertaker. Immediately, please." Inside, he was distraught, but it would not be proper for the servants to see his misery. He had to retain his composure at all costs.

Creighton Manor had recently been outfitted with telephone service. Only about a hundred nearby homes and businesses had the service. Fortunately, both the doctor and the undertaker had seen the necessity of being connected. Mrs. MacDonald lifted the earpiece then fluttered the hook up and down. This brought the operator on the line, obviously roused from her sleep on a daybed next to the switchboard.

"Hello, this is the Operator. Who should I connect you to?" the operator queried.

"Please connect me with Doctor Schultz. There's been an accident at Creighton Manor," Mrs. MacDonald said, the urgency in her voice clear.

Agnes Warfield, the Operator, did as she was asked and connected through to Doctor Schultz's line. Because of the lateness of the hour, Agnes could not resist the temptation to listen on the line as Flora MacDonald told the story to Schultz, who confirmed that he would be on his way in just a few minutes.

As soon as Doctor Schultz hung up the earpiece and ended the call, Mrs. MacDonald was once again fluttering the hook to signal Agnes again.

"This is the Operator. Who should I connect you to?" said Agnes once again, keeping to the standard script as she had been taught.

"Agnes, I know you were listening on the line, so you already know that Cora Mae Creighton is dead. I trust that you will keep this matter secret until Mr. Creighton officially announces it… Anyway, please also ring me through to Mr. Florio, the undertaker. He will need to come to Creighton Manor as well." The informality of the conversation between Mrs. MacDonald and Agnes Warfield was typical of the period: telephone operators and servants of wealthy customers generally knew each other by first name.

Because she had been called out for eavesdropping, Agnes Warfield remained formal in her response. "Yes, Mrs. MacDonald," she acknowledged as she placed the call to the undertaker, Carmine Florio.

Mrs. MacDonald repeated the same information to Florio that she had given Doctor Schultz. Florio, too, said he would be on the way in short order.

Doctor Schultz arrived first, followed by Mr. Florio a few moments later. Mrs. MacDonald quickly ushered the doctor upstairs to where Cora Mae's body lay. After a quick examination and pronouncing her deceased, he began to look for signs of trauma. Clearing the room of everyone except himself and Mr. Creighton, Schultz began a dignified examination that did not involve exposing any part of Cora Mae's body to the prying eyes of the males servants. It was his job as both the family physician and the County Coroner to do his best to determine the cause of death before the body was removed.

Schultz was meticulous in his approach to examining bodies of the deceased *in situ*. There was very little that escaped his practiced eyes. A more formal and intimate examination would take place before Cora Mae's body was made ready for burial – but he observed almost immediately that she had been barefoot at the time of her death, that she had recently washed her hair, and that there were burn marks on her left index finger and the sole of her right foot.

"Mr. Creighton," Schultz said, "I believe your daughter was electrocuted. That is my preliminary finding. If it is confirmed by my post-mortem exam, that is what will appear on the death certificate as cause of death."

Dr. Schultz summoned Mr. Florio upstairs and gave him instructions for moving the body to the mortuary. "She is not to be dressed for viewing until after I have completely examined her. I must do a head-to-toe examination to confirm my preliminary finding." There was absolutely no emotion in Dr. Schultz's voice. Just like J. Morris Creighton, Schultz had become expert at concealing his emotions, especially in cases such as this one where the deceased had been a lifelong patient.

"Mr. Creighton... Morris... I think it would be best if you left the room now so that Mr. Florio can do his work," Schultz said as compassionately as he could. "There are some things a father just wasn't meant to see, and this is one of them."

"Yes, of course…" Creighton replied absent-mindedly. The reality of his loss was beginning to set in. Returning to the library with Dr. Schultz close behind, J. Morris Creighton collapsed into one of the fine leather chairs. Burying his head in the palms of his hands, Creighton sobbed and wailed uncontrollably. Schultz knew that he should just wait it out until Creighton regained his composure.

"Morris," Schultz said, using his patient's first name as a show of compassion, "I can give you a sedative to help you sleep tonight. That is entirely up to you. I do recommend that you are in your bedchamber before I administer the injection, as its effects are rapid and quite dramatic."

Back on the second floor of Creighton Manor, Mrs. MacDonald was sending the staff back to their rooms. She wanted Cora Mae Creighton to retain her dignity, even in death. Thinking ahead to how distraught Emma Sue likely would become during the night, Mrs. MacDonald also assigned one of the senior maids to Emma Sue's room for the overnight hours after directing that a servant's cot be set up at the foot of the bed.

As he waited for his patient and friend to get ready for bed, Dr. Schultz filled his hypodermic syringe with a chloral hydrate formulation. He would administer the injection directly into a vein in Creighton's arms and remain with him until he was satisfied that Creighton was asleep and in no danger of apnea. Experience and research had shown Schultz that the danger of apnea from the sedative was greatest in the first thirty minutes after administration.

Down the hall, Florio called his assistant in from the mortuary wagon once all of the servants were out of view, Together, Carmine Florio and the assistant carefully removed Cora Mae's body from Creighton Manor and transported it to the Florio Mortuary and Funeral Home to await Dr. Schultz's examination.

Chapter Twenty-Seven: Schultz's Findings
After Cora Mae's Death

"I have completed a post-mortem examination of the remains of Miss Cora Mae Creighton, aged twenty-three, of this city. She died on June 24, 1911, and a preliminary cause of death was recorded as electrocution. Miss Creighton had been in my care since infancy and she was a healthy, fully developed woman at the time of her death.

A full dermal examination revealed no significant trauma to the trunk; however, there were burn marks on her extremities consistent with electricity entering the body from a live source and exiting the body at a ground. The point of entry was Miss Creighton's left index finger, and the ground point was the transverse metatarsal arch of her left foot. It should also be noted that she had apparently just taken a bath, as her hair was still wet when I arrived at Creighton Manor.

When the body was retrieved from Miss Creighton's residence at Creighton Manor, it was entering rigor mortis. This established the time of death not less than two hours before my arrival on the scene, which was just after midnight on the morning of June 25, 1911.

Schultz's details of the necropsy were thorough. His head-to-toe examination ruled out any sexual or blunt-force trauma. That eliminated Thomas Herrington Slater from the information he would turn over to the police.

After making the standard "Y" incision in the cadaver's chest and opening up the ribcage, Schultz made his next observation:

Most remarkable was the heart, which evidenced significant flaccidity caused by the electrical current. It was obvious that the heart had been in ventricular fibrillation for a considerable period of time before Miss Creighton expired.

The findings of the gross organ analysis were consistent with the preliminary cause of death established on the scene. These findings eliminated the need for a craniectomy and bilateral hemispherectomy.

Though the final cause of death is determined to be electrocution. However, it remains unclear if the death was caused by misadventure, negligence, or malicious intent by a party or parties unknown. A further examination of the electrical wiring of Creighton Manor, supervised by the local constabulary, is warranted."

Chapter Twenty-Eight: Panic
Late Summer, 1911

Dr. Schultz turned his findings over to the local sheriff's department and the Maryland State Police, neither of which had yet developed sophisticated forensic capabilities nor the technical expertise to investigate the case. Based on Schultz's assertion that there could have been suspicious circumstances, the two constabularies sought out an electrician to evaluate the wiring of Creighton Manor. That electrician was none other than Archibald "Sparky" Thompson, who had wired large portions of Baltimore City for electric service.

It took two full days for Sparky to inspect every electrical component in Creighton Manor. He determined that the electrician who wired the home had been competent and had done things as he would have done himself. Sparky blanched and nearly vomited when he discovered that there was some hardware, switches in particular, that obviously had come from the spoils at the General Electric plant in New Jersey, likely purloined and sold by John Garfield in his side hustle. He thought John Garfield's reach ended with his death; instead, there were still numerous components remaining in the inventories of electrical suppliers and hardware stores up and down the Mid-Atlantic region.

During the investigation of Garfield's vengeful misdeeds, Sparky had learned how to quickly identify the defective components: the small screws holding the contacts in place were loose to the point of falling out because the threading in the switch housing had stripped during assembly. Over time, the screws would simply fall out of their holes and allow the now free-floating switch contact to arc with between the live side and a ground. If a person was the conduit from the live side to the ground, the results had nearly always been fatal, as Dr. Mittford's investigation had proven.

The defect was a result of a manufacturing process and not caused by a willful act by an individual. John Garfield didn't know how the switches were defective, just that they were and that the defect could cause harm. As he said in his goodbye letter to Sparky, it was not his intent for anyone to be killed.

Cora Mae Creighton's death was reported in the Baltimore newspapers the next day. A week later, Dr. Mittford received his copy through the mail. Mittford had thought that his work was done now that John Garfield had been executed. After reading the account of Cora Mae Creighton's death, he realized that he couldn't have been more wrong.

The newspaper account included information, allegedly provided by Archibald "Sparky" Thompson, suggesting that defective components were widespread. Sparky didn't realize when he made the statement how much the media would twist his words. For newspapers of the period, facts and details were often exaggerated and rarely checked for accuracy. Garfield, the reporter wrote based on Sparky's words, had set electrification back by several years.

The sensationalized story quickly caused a panic among the servants of the well-to-do, making most of them fearful of even touching an electric switch or outlet. They did not want to be the next victim. Their employers, too, were reluctant to touch any of the switches for fear of meeting the same fate as Cora Mae Creighton. Some homes even reverted to candlelight rather than risk electrocution.

Mittford knew that Sparky had recently moved to into his own craftsman's cottage in Arbutus, a suburb of Baltimore, and that he now had a telephone. After reading the newspaper accounts of the Creighton Manor incident,

Mittford called Sparky, who answered almost immediately after a series of operators connected the trunk call.

"Sparky, it's Mittford here. Have you read the newspapers and the story about Cora Mae Creighton?"

"Yes, Doc... I have... The authorities and the rich people here are keeping me quite busy inspecting and repairing the wiring of their homes and businesses. I have more work than Seamus and I can handle," Sparky replied. "I thought this all ended with John Garfield's visit to "Old Smokey," but I guess I was wrong."

"We've certainly got our work cut out for us, don't we?" Mittford replied. "How are you finding out which of the switches or outlets are defective?"

Sparky explained, "I examined a few that I installed in Baltimore and compared them to the ones I have purchased directly from General Electric since Garfield's arrest. The defective items were, believe it or not, marked inside the housing with a scribed "X" to indicate they were unusable. Unfortunately, the scribe mark is very difficult to see. It would have been better if Edison had instructed his testers to smash the defective items with a hammer. The defect was pretty straightforward, though... Each bad part had stripped screw holes where the contacts were anchored.

This meant that the switch would self-destruct over time. Like a fuse on a stick of dynamite, if you will, and John Garfield lit the fuse."

"How many have you found so far that needed replacing?" Mittford asked.

"It's usually about one in every ten," Sparky answered.

"The newspapers are all over this, Sparky. They are scaring people with the exaggerated accounts and suggestions of danger," said Mittford. "Even people here in Essex County are worried and Edison has had to hire armed security guards to protect his workers."

"Besides Cora Mae Creighton, have you seen reports of any other deaths from electrocution?" Sparky asked.

"Fortunately, no. Nothing in any of the papers I have delivered here to the Essex Club. That's not to say there haven't been unreported incidents, especially from the poorer or Negro neighborhoods. Remember how little space Velma Smith got in the Baltimore paper?" Mittford reminded.

"Yes, sir... it's always the rich and powerful that get the most attention in the papers," Sparky lamented.

"I will be in Baltimore the day after tomorrow to offer my assistance to your investigation. You focus on inspecting and replacing the defective parts and I will document your findings," Mittford said. He knew that Sparky would be focused on getting the job done, not the forensic documentation that needed to be compiled to prevent another John Garfield.

"Doc, you have a place to stay while you are here. I have plenty of room. I don't have a wife... yet... and my house is more than big enough for the two of us," Sparky said with some excitement in his voice. He thoroughly enjoyed Dr. Mittford's company.

"No wife... yet... you say? Is there a prospective Mrs. Thompson in the wings?" Mittford asked.

"Not yet... but there could be. It's time for me to think about settling down. I've done enough traveling and living in hotels to last a lifetime," Sparky responded.

"I look forward to seeing you. Can you meet me at the St. Denis station?" Mittford asked.

"I know it well. I will be there," Sparky confirmed.

Meanwhile, across town, Thomas Alva Edison sat in his office. The rest of the staff had gone home for the evening, leaving him alone with his thoughts. He pulled an envelope from his desk drawer. It bore a return address of "Trenton State Penitentiary." Edison had held the letter for several months without opening it.

Edison knew that the content of the envelope was likely a letter from John Garfield – perhaps even his final letter as a living, breathing human being. Edison's opinion of Garfield had not changed. He harrumphed out loud, even though no one else was within earshot, "John Garfield deserved the punishment he got. He was a good-for-nothing and I should have fired him instead of keeping him on as a janitor,"

Eventually, Edison's curiosity got the best of him. He opened the letter, carefully unfolded it, and began reading. Dated the day before Garfield's execution, the penmanship was elegant and precise, written by a man in full possession of his faculties though his death was rapidly approaching.

After reading the letter, there was no doubt in Edison's mind that Garfield wished to exact revenge after he was gone. By Garfield's own admission, there were still numerous faulty switches in circulation, "and it will be nearly impossible to recover them all," Garfield wrote.

Recognizing that Garfield's actions could be ruinous for General Electric, Edison decided not to share the letter with anyone. Instead, he took a match and lit the letter, placing it in the metal trash can next to his desk. As he watched the paper burn, he muttered, "Good riddance!"

Epilogue: Six Years Later
200 Miles West of Baltimore

The Clarion – Herald

Wednesday, March 21ˢᵗ, 1917

Miss Jessica Wilcox of this city and daughter of City Hospital administrator Jeremiah Wilcox, MD, was nearly electrocuted just after the noon meal yesterday when she plugged a lamp into an electrical outlet in her father's home. The near-electrocution was accidental. It is fortunate that her younger sister, Angelica, was home with her when it happened.

An inspector determined that Doctor Wilcox's home and the block around it had recently been converted from Direct Current (DC) to Alternating Current (AC); Miss Wilcox, age 20, had just purchased the lamp from the local department store. She was unaware that the lamp was wired for DC and her father's house was now AC.

Miss Wilcox does not appear to have suffered any long-lasting effects. Although she remains in City Hospital for observation, she is lucid and quite coherent. She was, however, burned where the electricity entered and left her body. Doctor Wilcox, a widower, has taken a few days' leave of absence from his duties to care for his daughter.

That was what the public was told. The inspector, however, noticed that there was more to the near-fatal electrocution than met the eye. The switch that caused the shock to Miss Wilcox was defective: the screws holding the contacts in place were stripped and had come loose, causing a ground fault through Miss Wilcox's body.

The inspector, having moved west from Essex County, New Jersey, remembered the hysteria that followed the discover of John Garfield's misdeeds. In fact, the panic and sudden downturn in work for electricians, had driven him out of business. The inspector, not wanting to be responsible for causing another panic, intentionally left the observation of the loose screws out of his official report.

John Garfield's legacy lived on.

Author Notes

The process of electrifying the United States intrigued me after reading accounts of accidental electrocutions in newspapers from the first two decades of the Twentieth Century. One of those accidents nearly killed a distant cousin of mine, the daughter of Henry Mills Hurd, MD, the first administrator of Johns Hopkins Hospital in Baltimore. Dr. Hurd is presumed to be my first cousin, four times removed; our common ancestor is Thomas Hurd (1782-1851), of Connecticut and New York. Thomas was Henry's grandfather and my fourth great grandfather.

Using that 1917 accident as the end point for this book, I created a backstory that covered the travels of an itinerant electrician who was cast off from the General Electric company run by Thomas Alva Edison. I tried to keep the technical aspects of electrification as accurate as I could. However, the story predates licensing of electricians and inspections of installations, which don't appear to have come into play until around the start of World War I. Unfortunately, my research was stymied by the unresponsiveness of the International Brotherhood of Electrical Workers Union; despite reaching out to several "locals," I never received so much as an acknowledgement of my queries. I am sure they could have provided a much deeper and more accurate historical insight into the process of electrification, inspections, and licensing of electricians.

I did uncover a paper by Alfred Porter Southwick, DDS, about the invention of the electric chair, which most eastern states began using around 1905 instead of hanging. My research suggested that Southwick and Edison may have both claimed inventorship of the electric chair, as the first execution by the apparatus was that of William Kemmler in August of 1890. Kemmler's name comes up in articles about both Southwick and Edison. It turns out, though, that Edison was more interested in winning a disagreement with George Westinghouse on the relative benefits of DC vs. AC current than he was in extolling the virtues of a new means of execution.

Newspaper accounts of accidental electrocutions also informed the story line for this book. While the United States was being electrified, there were factions who were dead-set against electrification, citing accidental electrocutions as a counterpoint to progress. Regardless, individuals like the fictitious Doctor Robert Mittford quickly realized that electricity as a whole was far safer than the gaslights and open-flame lights of previous generations.

Both the St. Louis Motorcar Company and the Norwalk Touring Car Company existed. During the early days of the automobile and before Henry Ford's assembly lines, cars were handmade and produced by craftsmen in small establishments. Many of them went bankrupt once Ford made the automobile affordable for the working class. St. Louis Motorcar and the Norwalk Touring Car companies were two casualties of Ford's mass production.

The story lines passing through and around Baltimore, Maryland are accurate for the period. Baltimore's streetcar system was at the time one of the best in the country. Babe Ruth's father, George, did run several saloons – one of which is under what is now center field of Oriole Park at Camden Yards. Division Street is where Thurgood Marshall's family actually lived. Ruxton Heights to the north of the city and Lawyers Hill to the south are enclaves that were once the summer playgrounds of Baltimore's wealthy upper crust.

The now-removed Bloede (pronounced "Blerdeh") Dam was one of the first hydroelectric dams in Maryland; it was an "attractive nuisance" and the site of several drownings (despite strongly-worded warning signs) until its removal in 2019. I have ridden my bicycle and hiked near the dam's former location many times and it is now being returned to a natural state.

Also worthy of note is Baltimore's immigration terminal, which from about the time of the Civil War until the start of World War I rivaled New York in the volume of immigrants processed for admission. Baltimore excelled in one specific area: medical screening. Because ships came up the relatively tranquil Chesapeake Bay, inspections could begin before the ships reached port; I highlighted the process in "The Germans: Lineage Series, Book Six" and briefly touched on it again in this book when the Conatys arrived in Baltimore. As a further nod to my immigrant great-grandparents who were the basis for characters in Book Six, the German couple clearing immigration ahead of the Conatys were none other than August and Klara Fenstermacher, characters from "The Germans: Lineage Series, Book Six"

We believe, but can't confirm, that a Conaty family did enter the United States through Baltimore. This would have been an ancestor of one of Lineage Independent Publishing's other authors, Rebecca Conaty Bruce. In fact,

Seamus and Bridgit were the real names (used with permission) and they subsequently settled in Michigan as farmers.

Arbutus, where the fictitious Sparky Thompson finally settled, is another real location. It is a proud working-class suburb of Baltimore. In some ways, it remains the epitome of "Main Street, USA" with an annual festival, parades, and a very strong sense of community.

The final locations worth mentioning are the fictitious Creighton Manor and the J. T. Chalmers home. These homes were loosely based on the Craig Manor home in Chambersburg, Pennsylvania, which is now a well-maintained and beautiful bed and breakfast owned and operated by a very real Emily Secules. I used Craig Manor as the background source for how homes of the wealthy might have been constructed and laid out in the first decade of the Twentieth Century.

Acknowledgments

I would first like to recognize Lineage Independent Publishing's international team of authors: Lisa Talbott, G.B. Carmichael, Rebecca Conaty Bruce, and Lorna Hart. They have been my sounding board throughout the production of this book. I also need to give a shout-out to my friends Sarah Bomgardner and David Wilson, both of whom have reviewed different aspects of the book for readability. Then there's nonagenarian Elizabeth Talbott (Lisa's mother), who always provides relevant feedback and "color commentary." I hope I have her energy when I am in that decade of my life!

It goes without saying that my wife of over four decades, Sandy Hurd, has always been supportive of my efforts as an author and publisher. It is her unfailing support and inspiration that has pushed me through some periods of "writer's block."

Lastly, a huge shout-out to Emily Secules, owner of the Craig Manor Bed and Breakfast in Chambersburg, Pennsylvania. When I first had the idea for this book, I reached out to Emily (who was a neighbor when we were stationed overseas) and told her that her B&B was an ideal backdrop for the book. In fact, it is her photograph of Craig Manor that appears on the cover. During the early stages of my research, Emily provided a behind-the-scenes tour of Craig Manor and how it was laid out. The hand-carved staircase and sitting area were described in the Epilogue.

Michael Paul Hurd

Author/Publisher

Lineage Independent Publishing

Made in the USA
Columbia, SC
04 December 2022

72323982R10200